Fast Friends

#JustFriends Series - Book 3

MARIE COLE

*For D.B. for encouraging me to follow my dreams
- even if they don't involve selling real estate. XOXO*

Fast Friends

Chapter 1

Oh my god, this guy is so hot.

It was all I could think about as his lips trailed down my neck, his hands deliciously palming my breast and my ass. He groaned when we fell backwards together on the cab's backseat as Christmas music played through its cheap speakers.

"Excuse me. This is not the appropriate place for that behavior. Stop or I will have to terminate your ride."

The words barely registered but the sudden loss of his body on top of mine had not. It was my turn to groan.

"Sorry," he whispered with his lust-laden voice, pushing a chunk of his long dark hair back behind his ear. I'd probably been the reason it had become dislodged from his ponytail in the first place.

He helped me to sit up straight and then threw his arm over my shoulder, hugging me in close to his side. I stared at the rearview mirror to make sure we weren't being watched and smiled sweetly as my hand found the outline of him through his dark jeans. I couldn't wait to feel it outside of its confined space.

He leaned over and nudged my temple with his nose. "You better quit or we'll be walking." He nipped my earlobe, sending tingles of delight through my body. He let out a low growl of pleasure as my hand moved to his thigh.

"Walking isn't the exercise I really had in mind," I murmured.

"Me either, Princess," he replied.

"Mmm." I snuggled against the powerful man who was cradling me, trying to center myself. I'd had too much to drink. Too, too much. I closed my eyes and let the car gently sway us. Vaguely I was aware that Jesus probably wouldn't approve of my getting sloshed on the day of his birth. But I considered this a present to myself since I hadn't received any other gifts this year.

The taxi lurched to a stop, causing me to gasp softly. Rio chuckled beside me. I looked up and caught a brief glimpse of his amazingly beautiful smile before he was ushering me out of the warm cab and onto the street. I stared at his ass as he reached back into the cab to pay for the ride.

So tight. I just wanted to—

"Hey!" He chuckled as he spun around and swatted at my fingers, which were pinching him.

I giggled as he grabbed both my hands and pulled me against his warm chest.

"Hey," I said, my voice sounded weirdly sexy to my own ears.

He stared at me for a moment, his panty-dropping expressive blue eyes searching mine for something. Before I could ask what he was looking for, his lips came down on mine. It was as if something had exploded in my body and for the hundredth time that evening I wasn't sure if I was going to be able to walk when his arms eventually left my backside. He pulled away and I whimpered at the loss. His chuckle was deep and harsh.

"Just up a few stairs. Then I promise I'll strip you down. Piece by piece."

His words sent shivers through my body. I bit my lip to keep myself together. The last thing I needed was my body in a puddle on the sidewalk in front of his house. I paid no attention to my surroundings, my eyes focused solely on his ass. Oh my god. His ass. I couldn't wait to dig my heels into it.

I stumbled up the concrete stairs and watched as he pulled some keys from somewhere. Maybe that's what the little poking had been in the cab. I registered a little pain as I bit the inside of my mouth.

Shit.

My hands curled into fists as he fumbled with the key in the lock.

Hurry up, hurry up!

Finally, he got the lock open and pushed the door open. He waited for me to go first, which I thought was super charming, and I went inside. I glanced around quickly noting that it was a bit messy. But it didn't smell bad and I didn't see any critters. I pulled off my shoes, holding onto a white wall as I did so, my back towards most of the house. He was so heavenly to look at that I was having second thoughts. Maybe he was realizing his mistake. Maybe he was thinking that he shouldn't be with some slutty girl he met at the bar. Maybe...

My thoughts were interrupted by his lips. The sound of his keys hitting the floor barely registered above his sexy ass moaning and the excitement of my back hitting the wall. He stole my breath, my gasp swallowed by his delicious lips. The scratchiness of his short beard mixed with the gentleness of his hands on my hips was driving me crazy. My hands went to his pants, I didn't want to waste any more time. My body curved towards his, his belt jingling between us.

His pants fell just enough to open and reveal his cock struggling against the inside of his black boxer briefs. His hands started to roam after he removed my coat and let it drop to the floor. It pooled behind my feet. His hands continued their exploration, moving towards my tits which were aching for his touch. I groaned and ground myself against him as I lifted my hands up, helping him to get my shirt off.

"I can't wait to feel how you feel inside me."

"Just a little longer," his gravelly voice answered me as he lifted the shirt free. He kissed me once more and pulled me towards his couch, stripping my clothes from me, as promised, along the way.

"That's enough talking," I said as I stripped off his leather jacket and then his shirt and tossed them haphazardly across the room. I fell back with him onto the couch, my lips seeking his again. His hands pushed everything down his hips before he let his body come towards mine.

I groaned in frustration. Too slow! I shifted and pushed him down onto the couch and climbed on top of him. I kissed him, my center pressed against him. I gasped as he filled me. It was slow, sweet torture. His hands on my hips held me in place as he claimed me.

Chapter 2

Stacy

I woke up with a sharp gasp and groaned as my hand touched my forehead which was pounding louder than the thumping of the bass in the bar last night. My eyes raked over the ridiculously hot man lying beside me and slowly the night started coming back to me.

Oh god, what had I done?

This had been a mistake. Did I really want to be with a guy who took a total stranger to bed? He probably did this kind of thing all the fucking time.

Shit!

I pushed my hair back from my face and quickly tumbled out of his bed. What was I doing? Oh my god, oh my god! Elly was totally going to know that I boned him.

And so what if I had boned him? No, that wasn't the right attitude. This was so bad. I had just confessed to her before her open mic how much I wanted a stable guy. A good guy. A guy that I could take home to my mother and say, 'See! This is what a fucking good guy looks like, Mom. They aren't that hard to find!' But this wasn't that guy. This guy was in a band. He had so many tattoos he drew the eye towards him, and he probably had lots of casual sex while high on drugs. I didn't need that kind of guy.

Shit!

I crawled out of bed and tip-toed to his bathroom. After I cleaned myself up and swallowed some Tylenol I found in his cupboard, I crept back out to gather my clothes. I paused beside the bed and stared at him one last time. He was still sleeping. My fingers itched to move some of his long, dark wavy hair from his cheek. There was nothing I wanted to do more than climb back into bed with him. But I couldn't do that. He was bad news and forbidden. Still, I couldn't help myself as I snapped a quick picture on my phone before zipping out to his living room. I pulled on all of my discarded clothes in a hurry and made it safely out of his house.

It wasn't until I was a few houses down that I realized I'd forgotten my bra. Ah, well, something for him to remember me by. Or something for him to add to his collection, if he had one. Whatever.

As I walked down the street and called the number for a cab, I couldn't help but wonder how many other girls he'd been with, and I struggled to remember if we'd used protection.

"Jesus, Stacy," I reprimanded myself openly as I smacked myself on the forehead. I could have any number of diseases. What the fuck had I been thinking? Right. I'd been thinking that he was fucking sexy and that I wanted to have his babies. How fucked up was I?

I walked a few more blocks before the cab pulled up. My mind was on Elly as I rode home. I hope I hadn't messed up her chance at being in a solid band. I wasn't sure if Rio would call her. Hell, I wasn't even sure his band was legit. It was probably just a line, his way to get me into his bed. He had certainly been successful. He was charming, for sure. Too bad I wasn't going to speak to him again until I was fully committed and/or married to the man of my dreams. The kind of man who never had a one night stand and would never even see the merit of having one.

I paid the cab driver, tip and all, and did my walk of shame to my apartment. It was a downstairs studio apartment with an external door all its own, and it was smaller than tiny, but it was mine. And I had paid for it all on my own.

I didn't want to think about that right now either. I had work in two hours. Back to the grindstone for me.

***

Just after I got out of the shower I heard my phone go off. I snatched it up just before the last ring. "Hello?"

"Hey. Does your head hurt as much as mine does?"

I let out a breath I didn't know I'd been holding as Elly's voice registered in my brain. I couldn't believe I'd expected him to call.

"No. I took two Excedrin and my mother's magical hangover cure hours ago. Do you want me to tell you what it is? It's two parts V-8, two parts Sprite and—" Before I could say more Elly interrupted me.

"Oh my god! Stop!"

I grinned to myself as she moaned in agony on the other end. I pulled on my underwear.

"So what happened with you and Kent last night?" I asked, casually. They'd been really close last night. Really, really close. If it had been anyone but Kent I might have wondered if Elly had been too drunk to leave alone. But it was Kent, he was no stranger and too buttoned up to cheat on his fiancé. But I was pretty sure I hadn't been hallucinating.

Elly blew out a heavy breath. "I— I don't even want to talk about it. It was so stupid."

I gasped excitedly, pausing with my jeans pulled up to my ankles. "Did you guys—?"

"No! No. God."

I chuckled at her mortification as I yanked on my light blue sweater. "Not everyone is as free-spirited as I am, I guess."

"True, but in your defense that guy was pretty hot."

"I know, right?!" I sighed heavily and then she did the same. "I wonder if he's actually going to call you about his band."

"Eh. I don't know. Depends if you were a good lay or not, I'm pretty sure."

I couldn't hold back the laughter that was bubbling up in my chest. There was nothing like a best friend to put some humor into a horrible situation. "He'll definitely be calling you then." There was a slight pause before I spoke again, "Listen Elly, it's going to be alright. You'll find the right guy for you. Or Kent will wise up and get his head out of his ass. But until then you've got me. And I'm the best. So no worries, alright?"

"It's hard not to be upset. Last night he kissed me. And we almost..." Her voice wavered.

"God, he's such an idiot."

"What?"

"He's just so stupid. I'm sorry, I know he's your other bestie, or whatever, but seriously, Elly. You gotta get off his jock and stay away from him. He's not good for you." She was silent for a moment too long and I was worried that maybe it was too much honesty too soon. "I'm only saying this because I'm your friend and I don't want to see you go down the rabbit hole. You won't return a sane person."

"You're right. I know you're right," she said softly between sniffles. I could tell she had resolved to tell herself that, but I also knew the heart was crazy and usually wanted things it shouldn't have. Like soon-to-be-married men. "I'm going to go try and sleep this hangover off. I'll call you later."

"Okay. Later, boo. Feel better."

Oh, fuck. I fucked up. I rolled over and pinched the bridge of my nose as the realization hit me. Two years of sobriety down the fucking toilet. With my eyes still closed I replayed the evening in my mind. Two beers and I'd been as drunk as I used to get on half a bottle of whiskey.   Fuck.

I rubbed my face with my hands to try to rub away the stupid. It didn't work. I grabbed my cellphone and immediately dialed my number one.

"Rio. What's up?"

The voice on the other end of the phone would understand, I knew he would, but I still didn't want to have to say it.

"I, uh…" My throat constricted tightly. I coughed and tried to force out the words. Just say it, just say it! "I fell off the wagon last night."

There was a pause, a long one. It seemed endless. I pulled the phone away from my face to make sure he was still there on the other end.

"What happened, man?"

I rubbed at my forehead. I didn't want to tell him why. I didn't want to admit that I'd just felt like there was this hole in my life and I needed to fill it. I wasn't sure he'd understand since I didn't even really fucking understand it myself. There was something about Christmas that just made me feel so… alone. "I just fucked up."

"Alright. So why didn't you call me? We could've talked about it or hung out last night," Tom said, his calm voice soothing my frayed nerves and the rising panic and self-loathing I was feeling.

"It was Christmas, man. I didn't want to bother you and your family. And if I'm completely honest, I fucking hate Christmas and I wanted to have some fun and let loose. I wanted to feel like myself."

"Your old self. And how did that go? Did you have fun and let loose?"

"I didn't want to, at first. But then, I did. I took a drink and then more. And I let loose and had fun."

"With a woman."

"Wha… why would you assume there was a woman?"

"There is always a woman. Or a man depending on your preference."

"Are you saying I'm going to live the rest of my life fucking alone because women will trigger my alcoholism? That's some bullshit, Tom!"

"Rio, calm down. I'm saying you haven't had a drop to drink or a woman in your life for two years. You haven't tried dating while sober."

He had a point. I hadn't tried dating sober. And my first time meeting a woman who I was interested in just happened to be in a bar when I was begging for a reason to have a bender.

"Rio, are you okay today? Do you feel the urge to drink?"

I thought about it before I responded, "No. I'm okay today."

"Alright, if anything changes, if you feel that urge, then call me. I'm here for you."

"Thanks, Tom."

"Oh, and Rio?"

"Yeah?"

"Stay away from bars and women for a couple of weeks, okay? Make sure your head is on right first."

"Tom, come on. I was two years sober. Surely I can juggle a woman without the crutch of alcohol."

"I don't doubt you could, Rio, but you need to get your head straight before you try it. Trust me on this one."

I grunted in agreement and then hung up.

I rolled over and stared at the indent on the pillow next to mine. She had been there. I could still see her gorgeous face, her fiery red hair, and those green eyes of hers that seemed to see right into my soul. I grabbed the pillow and roughly turned it over, erasing any trace of her. It didn't matter. I didn't have the strength to be with her or any other woman. I wasn't ready yet.

***

"Hey, man! I was wondering when you were going to call and dish about the hot chick you went home with last night. Was she wild in bed? Frank and I were taking bets. Please tell me she wanted you to call her daddy," James said, a huge grin on his face, as I strolled onto the construction site.

"How the hell did you know I went home with a hot chick last night?" James was gone well before the texting extravaganza happened with Stacy.

"Frank made it to the bar just in time to see you sucking face with a girl as you squeezed her into the back of a cab. So you're not going to brag about how you went balls deep in that girl?"

"James. You're disgusting." I pulled my hair back and secured it with a band before putting my safety helmet on. "By the way, we're practicing tonight and hopefully auditioning a new singer."

"Fuck yes. Is it a woman? Is she hot? Oh, please!"

"Bandmates are off limits, James. You know the rules."

"Yeah, yeah. But I'll still get to stare at her ass the whole time we're playing. Being the drummer has its perks, for sure."

I was glad that James wasn't talking about Stacy. I was barely containing myself while he was talking about her friend. She had seemed nice enough from what little time we'd spent together.

"Anyway. Seven, my place."

"Cool. Do I need to fill the fridge?"

The mere thought of a beer made my mouth water and my head ache.

"Uh, no. Listen…" I exhaled slowly. I wasn't a pussy. I could do this. "I kind of fucked up last night so I need a clean house for a while."

There was a long pause while I guessed James digested what I'd said. "How long had it been again?"

"Two years. Nearly."

"Fuck. Alright, no booze it is. I'll even make sure I acid out my mouth with that mouthwash shit before I come over so you won't have to smell it on me. I'll be there."

"Thanks."

It was a relief to have such a supportive, if not immature, friend. James had been there through the worst of it and he and his family had dusted me off, nursed me back to health, and given me a job. I would probably be dead if it hadn't been for them.

***

After work, I dialed Elly's number.

"Hello?" Her voice was extremely unsure as she'd answered.

"Hey, Elly. I don't know if you remember me but this is Rio. I met you and Stacy at the bar last night. She said you were a singer and I wasn't fucking around when I told her we needed one. Are you available to audition tonight?"

"Uh...tonight?"

"It's cool if you already had plans. The band practices four times a week. It would be nice to have vocals but we've been jamming without them just fine for a few weeks now."

"It's not that. I just don't have a ride. Can we do it tomorrow night?"

"I can give you a ride, if you want."

"No offense, but I don't really know you that well."

"Alright, good point. It's always good to be safe."

Fuck. If she wasn't going to come by herself then that would mean she was going to bring someone else and I was sure I knew who she was going to ask. I hoped like hell she was still friends with that dude from the bar last night and that it was him she was planning on bringing and not Stacy.

"What time tonight if I can find a ride?"

"Uh, seven. I'll text you my address and you can text me and let me know if you can make it. Cool?"

"Yeah. I'll be in touch, Rio."

After hanging up, I went to the shower. I needed to clear my head.

Alone with my thoughts I had to admit to myself that last night wasn't just a slip up. It was me avoiding thinking about my past. I was trying to drown myself in the bottle and avoid confronting my past which is what fucked me up in the first place and turned me into my father. I refused to let myself be him and this was the first step. I was an alcoholic and I always would be. Step one to my long road to recovery was to wipe clean the people from my life who were going to push me into that lifestyle again.

A big one came to mind.

A woman who had awakened my body. A woman whose voice I hadn't been able to shake from my head all damn day as I hammered nails into two by fours in the freezing December air.

Stacy was off limits. She would do nothing but cause me trouble and lead me straight to the bottle. She was too fun, young, and carefree. I needed to get my head right first and probably when that happened she'd be swept up in someone else. She seemed like the kind of girl who didn't wait around. But most of all, she was the kind of girl who didn't need to be tied down by a broken guy like me.

Chapter 3

Stacy

I was most of the way to my mama's trailer when my phone rang. I glanced at the caller ID and Elly's number flashed at me.

"Goddammit," I muttered as I reached for it. I wondered what was going on now. It had only been an hour since I'd last talked to her. I hit the button and pressed the phone to my ear. "Holla."

"Stacy, Rio just called me and he wants me to audition tonight. I don't really want to go to some strange man's house, no offense, alone. And after last night I can't ask Kent and my mom isn't answering her phone so I was wondering…"

If I hadn't been going sixty miles an hour I probably would've been pounding my head against the steering wheel at that moment. "Um… sure. What time? I'm almost to my mom's."

"At seven. Can you make it back by then?"

I glanced at the clock. I had three hours. "Sure, I'll cut this thing with my mom short and head back. You owe me one. Gas ain't cheap."

"I've got the gas money covered. Thanks, Stacy! I'll see you soon."

"Okay, bye Els." I ended the call and threw the phone back into my purse. goddammit. I was going to have to see him again. It would be fine. I was a strong woman and he was a player. He would probably just flirt with me or pretend it had never happened at all. I was totally cool with either of those situations if it meant it would be easy to keep him at arm's length.

I pulled up to the trailer and got out of the car. I'd made sure I wasn't wearing anything too flashy. I didn't want to attract the attention of any of my neighbors or my mom's husband. I knocked on the door and stood back, waiting for an answer. I took a step back when the door opened and smiled as I stared up at my mom.

She had been gorgeous when she was younger. She'd thought she'd have time to pursue her dreams once I got older but that was before my father ran out on us and left her with no way to find him and no money. She never left her crappy hourly job and continued to bounce from man to man as they wormed their way into her life.

"Hey mama." I stepped in and gave her a big hug. Her arms wrapped around me too and we swayed for a moment before I stepped back. "I'm sorry I missed Christmas." The truth was that she'd been working on Christmas while her good for nothing husband stayed home watching TV.

She pushed my hair back from my face just liked she'd always done and smiled. "That's okay, baby girl. You're home now. Do you want something to drink?"

"No. And I have to get going real soon. I forgot that I'd promised my friend that I would take her somewhere. She just called me to remind me. She knows how absent-minded I can be." It was a white lie but I didn't want her husband to open his mouth about it.

Said husband, Hank, was on the recliner in the corner. I tried not to shudder as his eyes raked over the pair of us. I could only imagine what was going through his perverted mind.

"How kind of you to drive all this way for a drive-by hello. Sounds like you just wanted to come get your presents and run, girl." He laughed alone as his joke fell flat.

I forced a smile and looked back to my mom, "We can do presents another time soon, maybe I can come for New Year's?"

My mom frowned a little as she pushed her hair back from her face. "Well, that sounds nice, Stacy, but I'm working New Year's Eve too. You know how the holidays are."

I nodded, I did. The holidays were very busy for her. "I'll come back again before my last semester starts."

"What are your plans after graduation, baby girl?" Hank asked as he muted the TV and turned his full, unwanted, attention to me.

"I'm going to be interning. So money is going to be tight for me for a little while."

Hank scoffed, "Money's going to be tight? You need to start earning some money so you can pay your mama back for all the money she wasted on you when you were younger."

I glanced at my mother who was shaking her head in disagreement but not speaking up for herself. My eyes flicked back to Hank. "The interning is the key to getting a good job come the end of summer."

"You got it all figured out, don't you?" he retorted.

"And so do you, don't you? When are you going to get off your ass and stop mooching off my mama and get yourself a fucking job?"

My mom gasped as I shook my head and held my hands up in defeat. "I'm sorry, mama, but it's true. He needs to pull his weight around here. If he really loved you he'd get himself a job and let you stop working yourself to death." I glared at Hank before holding out a tiny little box to my mom. "Merry Christmas, Mama." I pressed my lips to her cheek before stepping out of the trailer once more. For once I wish she'd keep my gift instead of returning it but I knew as well as she did that if she didn't return it Hank would take it while she was at work and pawn it. I knew, between us, that it was the thought that counted anyway.

I got into my car and shut the door behind me with a huff. This is exactly the life I wanted to avoid. I did not want to grow up to be my mama. I was going to have something better.

Elly and I drove in silence to Rio's house. She was nervous because she was going to be singing with a group of guys whose only agenda was to judge if she was good enough. I was nervous because I was going to have to face Rio again.

The music drowned out my thoughts until we arrived at the house that I wasn't sure I could ever forget, even if I wanted to. No Stacy, he's trouble. In another ten years he'll be as washed up and useless as Hank.

I glared at Rio's door as if it had deeply offended me and then looked at Elly who was still nervously wringing her hands in her lap. I chuckled at her when her eyes met mine. "Elly, come on. They're a bunch of rock dudes. You've got this."

She nodded though she didn't look too sure of herself. "Yeah, I got this," she tried to reassure herself.

She got out of the car and I followed, my stomach twisting in knots the closer we got to the front door.

Shit.

Shit.

Shit.

Elly rang the doorbell and we both stepped back and waited for someone to appear in the doorway. I looked around as we waited and the sound of drums and electric guitar were trying to escape through the walls of Rio's house. "They probably can't hear the door. Should we just go in?"

She shrugged her shoulders and tried the doorknob. It turned and we entered the house. The volume increased dramatically as soon as we stepped in. We followed the music down the hallway and stopped in the doorway of a sunken in living room which had been prepped for band rehearsal. We waited and watched until they noticed us. They were so lost in the music. My eyes went to Rio and stayed there. Beads of sweat started to pop up on his forehead. His face was focused on the strings he was so skillfully playing. I blushed as my body remembered just how good those fingers felt on my skin.

Before I could let my thoughts go further away I waved my hands, trying to get their attention. Rio looked up and his fingers fumbled.

I looked down at my bloodied finger. "Fuck me," I muttered as I sucked the blood from the small wound on my thumb. I glanced around for the pick I'd dropped briefly before setting my bass down. "Take five, guys. I gotta bandage this shit up and get a new pick. Lost it." I didn't waste any time getting out of the room. Was she trying to show up here and see me on purpose? I didn't want to have to be a dick but if she didn't stay away I was going to have to be an asshole. I couldn't risk another slip up.

I didn't have to brush past the two, they got the hell out of my way as I made my way to my bathroom. I opened the cupboards and started to search for something to calm the throbbing that was quickly accelerating in my finger.

I smelled her before I saw her. I glanced up and saw her leaning in my doorway, her arms and ankles crossed.

"What the hell are you doing here?" I asked gruffly, hoping to scare her off. I glanced up, it hadn't worked. Fuck.

"Elly needed a ride. I'm said ride."

"You're fifteen fucking minutes late. Do you think your time is more important than ours?" I saw something resembling sadness cross her features before she put her mask back in place.

"I don't. I was driving as fast as I could without getting a ticket. I was in Jonesboro."

"What the fuck were you doing there? Looking for another bed warmer?" I clenched my jaw, the words came out before I could stop them. I didn't give a damn. I didn't want to, but I kind of did.

"Having a little Christmas with my mama."

She was visiting her mom and I was giving her shit about it. Jesus, I was an asshole. I stopped my shuffling and looked at her. "Sorry."

She shrugged her shoulders and opened one of the drawers I'd already shuffled around in. She pulled out a bandage and held it up for me to inspect. I took it, our fingers brushed momentarily and the chemistry between us went right to my pants. "Did you wake up on the wrong side of the bed?"

I smiled as my eyes met hers. "Maybe if you'd have stuck around you would know the answer to that question."

"Oh, is that why you're so grouchy?"

I made quick work of applying the bandage and ditched the trash before meeting her eyes again, "Nope. It might surprise you but I'm used to girls tucking tail and running the other way."

She scoffed, "I'm not surprised at all. Most girls aren't looking for a simple roll in the hay. Most girls want more."

Is that what she wanted? More? It didn't matter. I couldn't give it to her. I met her eyes again as I took a step towards her. She took a step back, looking nervous. Interesting. "So, are you doing anything after this?"

She rolled her eyes and waved me off as she moved towards the door. "Save your breath. I'm not interested." The way she hunched away from me said something altogether different.

"Okay, Princess. I was just curious if Elly was going to need a ride home."

Her eyes widened in surprise at my slight rejection before she could cover her face up again. "I was planning on staying."

I bandaged my finger, my eyes looking to her back and forth as I wrapped the sticky plastic around my appendage. I went to my dresser and grabbed a new pick before following after her.

Elly was getting along nicely with the guys as I reentered the band room. They were laughing until their eyes fell onto me. I felt like such a party pooper. My bad mood must have been embedded on my face.

"Hey. You guys ready to start again?" I forced a smile I wasn't feeling as I picked my bass up once again.

James snickered, "I was born ready."

Elly cleared her throat and cradled the mic in her hand before looking over her should at us. "What are we singing?"

"Singer's choice, darlin," I said.

She nodded, "Alright, how about "Two Princes?""

We all nodded to each other before starting rocking out once again. I already loved her taste in music, it was a song that was rock enough for us and gave each of us a chance to show off our talents. With the exception of me, of course. Bass guitar was difficult to make shine.

I kept my attention on my fingers, the other instruments, and Elly's voice. She was good, Stacy hadn't lied. Her voice was sultry and smooth and she had awesome range. We played a few more songs, each taking a turn recommending the next song on the playlist. Stacy stood in the doorway all the while, her arms and ankles crossed as she bobbed her head along with the beat. She was smiling, enjoying it.

Once we'd each gone around I pulled the bass from my shoulder and set it down. I approached Elly as I stuffed my hands into my pockets. "Well," I said as I looked over her eager and hopeful face, "I think we have ourselves a new lead singer."

She let out a scream before grabbing me and hugging me tight. She bounced off of me and then went around and hugged the other two. I grinned seeing the delight on James' face. My eyes turned back to Stacy who was smiling for her friend and still standing there in the doorway.

"So are you going to be bringing Elly to practice four times a week?"

She frowned, "Really? You guys practice four times a week? Isn't that a bit excessive?"

"You don't become good at something unless you keep at it."

My eyes moved down her body as she uncrossed her arms and my eyes zeroed in on her nipples. My mind clouded with sex visions. Me pressing her against the wall, my mouth around the tip of her breast. I growled the thought away and met her eyes which looked rather serious. Did she know what I was thinking?

Fuck.

"Like how to pick women up at a bar?"

I felt anger starting to creep in at her implication that I was some sleazy prick–again. "More like how to sneak out of a dude's bed before he wakes up."

Chapter 4

Stacy

I was still livid from what Rio had implied about me. He was just firing back the only ammunition he had. I tried to push my anger aside for Elly's sake. I glanced over at her and took in her pasted on smile. She was going to be smiling like that for weeks.

I leaned forward and turned the heat down as we drove along the road. New Year's Eve was a time that Elly and I usually had dinner with her mom and it was coming up fast.

"What time should I be at your mom's?"

Elly looked a little confused, "What are you talking about?"

"For New Year's? Or are we not doing that this year? It's cool if we're not, I'll find a party to go to or something."

Elly laughed. "Stacy! That's the day Kent is getting married, remember? You're going to be my plus one, aren't you?"

"Oh, right." My face dropped as I looked over her face. She tried to pretend that it didn't still affect her but I knew that it did. I knew her little heart was breaking at the thought of her best friend getting married to someone that wasn't her.

I didn't really know Jen personally but I knew what Elly had told me of her. I wasn't impressed.

"So you're taking Kent out for his bachelor party?"

"Yep! I don't have much time to plan it but I'm sure it will all come together."

It was my turn to laugh. "I'm sure. You're so anal when it comes to scheduling."

"Shush." She smiled as she wrapped her arms over her chest and shrugged her shoulders. "I'm going to make sure it's a night he'll never forget."

"So you're going to show up at his house wearing nothing but a big red bow? Because I'm sure that's a night he'd never forget."

Elly shifted in her seat uncomfortably and I inwardly cursed myself. "Damn, Elly, I'm sorry." I sighed softly. "My head is somewhere else."

"Yeah? With sexy Rio?"

"Pft. Ew. He's the epitome of a bad boy rock star. I'm not going to get involved with that."

"Again, you mean."

I shifted my seat and tried really hard to keep the memories of Chance at bay. Visions of him moving against some blonde headed girl in the back of his truck swam through my brain. I shook it away and focused on the approaching concrete.

"Right. Again. I need a change, Elly. I need to find a good guy. Someone slower paced. Less dangerous. Someone who makes me warm inside."

Elly stared at me and nodded. "Good luck with that. Thanks for coming to my rescue."

I grinned. "Anytime, Elly."

***

I arrived at my studio apartment and threw my purse on the little table I had by the front door before kicking off my boots and coat. They fell in a pile near the door. I glanced in the direction of the bathroom and my fingers twitched by my side as my eyes fell on the new candles Elly had gotten me for Christmas. I sighed dreamily as I walked that way. I turned on some soft tunes and the sound of water cascading from the faucet filled in the background.

As I soaked in my tiny tub, my mind wandered to my ideal man. He was as far from Rio and Chance as could be. He would be sweet and hold doors open for me. He would be pre-med or a business major or something like that. He would do volunteer work in his spare time. He would definitely have a dog. A golden retriever.

I smiled as I pictured myself and Mr. Perfect. We would go out for walks instead of hanging out in seedy bars. We would go shopping for groceries instead of booze for the after parties. We'd sleep in until noon because we enjoyed each other's company so much, not because we were so hung over we couldn't bear the thought of getting out of bed to do anything. We would have quiet Friday nights watching movies and eating popcorn.

The thought was so cozy and comforting. There was only one problem. Where the hell would I find Mr. Perfect?

The next morning I was standing in line waiting for the barista to take my coffee order when I felt my phone buzz in my pocket. I reached into my back pocket and felt something meet with my elbow. I spun around, hearing a loud grunt, and saw a guy stand up, holding his nose with both hands.

I gasped as I realized that I'd just elbowed the poor guy right in the nose. "Oh my god! Are you okay?"

He nodded and gingerly touched his nose before putting his hands down. "Yeah, I'll live. Good thing I've just come from my family Christmas portrait."

When his hands fell I was able to see just how handsome he was. He had a square jaw, blazing brown eyes and perfectly kissable lips. My eyes moved down further and took in his sweater/button down shirt combo and his khaki pants. Bingo! Here was Mr. Perfect and I'd just elbowed him in his perfect nose!

"I still feel really bad. Can I buy you a coffee or something?"

He chuckled and shook his head, "No. My mom would have a fit if she knew I'd let a beautiful woman buy me a coffee. Let me buy yours instead."

"I..." I had to process that for a minute. Did he just offer to buy the girl who nearly sent him to the hospital with a broken nose coffee? And mentioned his mother? Without shame or name-calling? "You really don't have to."

"It would be my pleasure. Please."

It was his manners and the half smile on his lips that made me give in. "Okay, I'd love that. Thanks."

He offered me his hand. "I'm Jordan."

I took it and tried to shake but he brought my hand to his lips and pressed a soft kiss there. I felt my cheeks blushing. Likes to charm the ladies with kisses to the hand? Definitely not a bad boy. "Stacy."

"Stacy. Nice to meet you. Did you have a merry Christmas?"

I stepped up beside him so that we could talk and move in line at the same time. "Um, I guess so. I was working." And banging a random dude. Oh god! I needed to stop thinking about him!

"Working? What do you do for work? Actress? Model?"

Before I could stop myself, I rolled my eyes at his cheesy line. "No. I'm a waitress."

"Yeah, I can see that. I bet you make great tips."

"Yeah, I guess. It's enough to get me by."

"Are you going to school?"

"Yeah, I'm an accounting major." I smiled as I looked over his handsome face. "And how about you? What's your major?"

"Oh, I'm finished with school. I graduated last year. Philosophy major."

Okay, so he wasn't a business major but at least he had a degree. That earned him some more brownie points.

"Philosophy, huh? What kind of job did you land with that one?"

He rubbed the back of his neck before shooting me a sheepish grin, "Well, it's been tough. My mom suggested I get a teaching license. I'm glad that I did, I'm teaching high schoolers. It's low stress and entertaining."

"You're probably a big hit with the high school girls."

I grinned at the blush that colored his cheeks.

"I try not to break too many hearts."

"I bet."

So far Jordan was about as close to the ideal perfect guy as I was likely to find on a Sunday morning. Ask and ye shall receive, right? I had to make sure I didn't let him get away without letting him know I was interested in something more and our time was quickly running out.

We stepped up to the counter and ordered. While we waited I continued our conversation and went in for the kill. "So, do you by any chance have plans for Thursday?"

He looked up at the ceiling in thought for a moment before looking back at me, a grin on his lips, "You know, I don't. The date with one of my high school students just cancelled on me." He held his hand out for my phone, "I'll give you my number and we can make plans."

I handed it over and watched as he typed in his info before giving it back. I slipped it into my back pocket and grabbed my coffee. "Sounds good."

The next few days were filled with work shifts and Thursday afternoon I found myself in Forever 21, trying to find something for my date with Jordan. We were going to go walking around downtown for a bit before snagging some dinner at this cozy little Indian restaurant.

I hummed to myself as I flipped through the clothes on the rack. I touched my face and realized I was smiling. I'd been doing that a lot since running into Jordan. We'd been texting back and forth for the past few days and I was anxiously waiting for four to roll around.

I grabbed a few things and was headed to the changing room when my phone started to ring. I glanced at the caller ID and picked it up when I saw that it was Elly.

"Hey girl, how did the bachelor party go?" There was a long pause on the other side of the phone and I pulled it away to make sure I was still connected. "Elly?" I put the phone back to my ear with a frown. "Elly? What's wrong?"

"We slept together."

My grip tightened in the clothes I was holding. "You slept with Kent?"

"Yes," she said, her voice quivering, sounding like tears that must have been welling up in her eyes.

"Okay... this is big." I looked around for somewhere to put the clothes I'd selected and ditched them quickly on the checkout counter before walking towards the exit of the store. "Do you need me to come get you? Where are you?"

"I'm walking towards my mom's. I just got a call from Jen too. Her band dropped out and she asked if I would step in. Kent had told her about my new band. I felt so guilty for what I'd done that I said yes. Without thinking about it. I need to call Rio and get everyone together so we can practice. We can't go in front of all those people without..."

"You need to stop worrying about that right now. I'm coming to your mom's and then I'll drive you to Rio's. Do you want me to call him?" I pressed my lips together as soon as the words were out.

Please say no. Please say no.

"No, I'll call him."

I breathed a heavy sigh of relief. "Okay. I'll be there soon."

I hung up the phone and ran to my car. Elly and Kent sleeping together was huge! I knew they'd done it once before but the way Elly had made it sound it was a mistake and a one-time thing. But here they were and they'd done it again. I ground my teeth. I could kill him for doing this to her. He was getting married tomorrow and he thought it would be okay to have his kicks with Elly just before tying the knot? It definitely was not okay. I paused. What if he wasn't going to get married? What if his kissing Elly and sleeping with her was his way of trying to get her to object to it all? To confess her feelings for him finally?

Another heavy sigh left me. There was no way she was going to do that. He was getting married. It was going to be up to him to make any big confessions he might want to before committing his life to another woman.

I parked in the street and made my way to the front door. I waited only a minute after knocking before Elly's mom answered. She smiled when she saw me and immediately opened her arms. I stepped in and gave her a hug. "Hi, Stacy! How are you?"

"I'd be better if ..." I paused again. Elly probably hadn't told her mother. "If this whole wedding business was over with. I'm ready to get back to school. Is Elly here?"

Her mom gave me a disbelieving look before looking at the stairs behind her. She turned back to me and pulled me all the way into the house. She shut the door behind me. "I think I heard her come in. You can go on up there and check. I was just finishing up some bacon on the stove."

I could smell it faintly. I nodded and headed up the stairs as her mom went back into the kitchen. When I got to her door I knocked and then entered. Elly was pacing, her phone to her ear.

"Rio, I know, I'm sorry. But it's money. Good money. And we could use the practice anyway. Please, please, please. This would mean so much to me."

I waved and then sat down at her desk as I waited for her conversation to be finished. Her room, filled with rock band posters and inspirational sayings, didn't match her anymore. I glanced around and saw nothing but teenage dreams. On her nightstand was a framed picture of her and high school Kent, arms around each other, dressed like a couple of storm troopers. They were such nerds.

Elly let out a loud sigh of relief. "Thank you! Okay, I'll be there. Thanks." She disconnected the call as she moved to stand by me. "I need a ride to Rio's house."

I nodded but didn't move. "Do you want to talk about this Kent thing first?"

She shook her head, her body tensing at the mention of his name, "Nope. He used me because I was convenient. There isn't anything else to say about it."

I frowned. "How do you know he was only using you? I've seen you two together, I know that he-"

She cut me off, "Because he told his mom that there was nothing going on. And he went to brunch with Jen this morning. And here we are. I need to move on and stop drooling over the untouchable boy next door. I need to leave it all in the past and when I see them get married I will know, finally, that the 'Elly & Kent' chapter is closed."

I stared at her hard for a long moment. She was trying to convince herself, that much was obvious. And she was hurt. I wasn't going to press her now but I was going to keep an eye out for her. I'd be her wing woman at the wedding and make sure that Kent didn't get the chance to hurt her again.

"Okay. Chapter closing. Let's get you to band practice so you can wow the crap out of Jen."

***

We arrived at Rio's after a rather quiet ride. We got out and headed up to the door. When she rang the bell I smiled. "So I'll come get you in a little while?"

"You're not staying?"

The worry on her face tugged at my heart.

"I wasn't planning on it but... if you really want me to stay then I will."

"Please, please, please?" She grabbed onto my wrist and pulled it towards her heart. I offered her a smile as I gave her hand a squeeze.

"Okay. I'll stay."

She was about to say something, probably thanks, but the door opened. Rio's six foot four inch sexy-as-sin body stood there. He appeared rather grumpy but judging by the few times I'd seen him sober, this was nothing out of the ordinary.

"What is she doing here?" he asked, his stunning blue eyes locking onto me. She was me.

"Stacy's my ride. She won't be a bother." Elly shot Rio a soft smile and his eyes looked over her face. His resolved melted the instant he looked at her tear-stained eyes.

"Come on in." He reluctantly stepped back to let us enter. Once the door closed behind us he pointed a long, commanding finger towards the living room. "TV is in there. Help yourself."

"Thanks." I watched as they walked away and just as I entered his kitchen, the music started up. I groaned. There was no way I was going to be able to drown them out. I set my coat and keys on the kitchen counter and then started meandering around his house.

Chapter 5

Rio

I motioned for the band to keep playing as I moved out of the room. The set list for this wedding was fucking ridiculous. The bride had the most mainstream taste in music I'd ever seen. The woman must have listened to the Top 40 and nothing else. The only saving grace to this were the important songs we were supposed to be playing for the first dance and shit.

I needed a break to use the bathroom and as I walked into my room I was stopped short by the sight of Stacy standing by my dresser. She was staring at the picture of my family that had been tucked into the top drawer of my dresser.

"See something you like?"

The sound of my voice snapped her out of her trance and her eyes fell on me. Instantly I felt my body react to it. She cleared her throat as she pointed to the picture.

"Are these your parents? Your sister?"

"Yup." My feet were moving in her direction, taking me directly towards her, like a moth to a flame. I stood directly behind her, looking over her shoulder at the picture in question. I already knew what it looked like. It was ingrained in my memory. It was taken just before everything in our lives went to shit.

"That's not how I imagined you looked when you were younger."

I scoffed. In high school I was an outcast and it showed through in this picture of us huddled together with Santa Claus. I was dressed all in black, including the black trench coat. My hair was greasy and short. Even though I was an outcast at school I fit in with my family. Or had before it'd been destroyed.

"Your sister is very pretty."

I turned Stacy around before her eyes could scan over my sister's image any longer. I didn't want to talk to Stacy about her. It was too painful. I didn't want to be reminded of it right now. "What the hell do you think you're doing going through my shit?" I grabbed the picture and stuffed it back where it had come from. The drawer closed with a loud slam that caused her body to startle. She looked guilty as hell and I was glad. She should feel bad for going through a man's personal shit. Her eyes avoided mine, searching the room until they landed on my alarm clock on my nightstand.

"Oh shit! Is that the time?"

"Yeah. Why? Gonna turn into a pumpkin at four?"

"No, I'm going to be late for my date!"

"Your date, huh?" I acted way cooler than I was feeling at that moment. This woman was a whirlwind of drama.

Her eyes flicked over me disapprovingly. "Yes. He's a nice guy."

"Oh, yeah, I'm sure of it." I moved away and went into my bathroom, closing the door behind me before I said something that would cause her to drag Elly out of my house and keep her away from me forever. I hadn't known Elly for very long but I already felt protective of her. She reminded me a little of my sister.

When I came out of the bathroom Stacy was gone, only her scent left behind. I took a deep whiff before moving back towards the rehearsal room. I grabbed my bass and got right back into it. We were onto playing another terrible song. I grit my teeth as I tried to memorize notes I'd hoped I would never have to hear again. This was for Elly. For the ghost tears I'd seen on her cheeks when I'd opened the door. I didn't know what this meant to her exactly but I knew it meant a lot.

***

It was late when we decided we had enough of a grasp of the material to call it a night. I handed out pillows and blankets before moving back to my room. Elly was coming out of the bathroom as I was in the middle of making my bed.

"Hey. I figured you could have the bed. You'll be the one everyone's eyes will be on tomorrow night."

She smiled softly and helped me make the bed.

"Thanks."

Stacy and the idea of her date had been eating at me all night. I knew I shouldn't be so damn curious because I was not on the market for a woman, especially not Stacy, but I couldn't help but ask. And I'd be tossing and turning all night if I didn't try my damnedest to find out more. Now I finally had Elly alone and I could ask her for more information.

"So, this dude that Stacy is dating...is that a new thing or...?" I let my words fade out and watched her face until she looked at me.

"It's a new guy, I guess. I didn't even know she was going on a date. If I would've known I wouldn't have begged her to stay."

So she hadn't wanted to stay? Of course she hadn't. I was the bad news she wanted to stay away from. We both knew that. It didn't make me feel any fucking better about it.

"Cool. Well, goodnight. Let me know if you need anything."

"Goodnight, Rio. Thanks for the bed."

I rubbed the back of my neck as I left my bedroom, a pillow in my hand. I sprawled out on the floor, grunting as I tried, and failed, to get comfortable. My mind wandered back to Stacy. To tasting her that night. To her smile, her laugh. Her scent.

I groaned as I turned, trying to discourage my dick from waking up. I didn't like that I was so far gone when it came to her. But I was glad that this new guy hadn't had a chance to get too far under her skin. Her body still reacted to mine. And for some reason I didn't understand I wanted to make her do it again. And again. And again. I wanted her to look at me with the admiration I'd seen the other night. I wasn't sure how I was going to bring them back. But I was.

***

I tugged at the damn bowtie which was slowly trying to strangle the life out of me. I sighed as I stared at myself in the mirror. I looked like a stranger, a fucking handsome stranger. I slicked back my hair and put it into a ponytail and then went to the living room where the other guys were in equally fancy garb. They looked just as uncomfortable as I did. I couldn't help but chuckle.

"Shut the fuck up, Rio," James grumbled as he got up and headed for the door.

"Dude, come on, it's just for a few hours. Maybe it will help you get laid tonight," I said as he passed by.

"It fucking better," he grumbled before climbing into his car.

Frank and I exchanged looks of amusement before leaving the house ourselves.

"He's going to be in a pissy mood all night. Such a diva."

I busted a laugh as we climbed into the van.

***

When we arrived we shrugged out of our tux jackets and started to set up our instruments on the stage. I checked my phone and frowned when I noted the time. The gig was going to start in an hour and I still hadn't heard anything from Elly since she'd left my house in the morning. She'd said she needed to go shopping and that she would meet us at the wedding. I shot her a quick text and then shoved my phone back into my pocket.

James stepped back and admired his handiwork before heading towards one of the bars set up along the perimeter of the room.

When I was sure it was as good as it was going to get I put my jacket back on and followed after him. A drink would be nice right now. I leaned against the bar as James chatted up the bartender and pulled my phone from my pocket. Nothing new. I sighed and put it away. I glanced around the large room and shook my head. I tugged at the bowtie once more before pushing off the bar.

"James, we got thirty minutes. One drink, okay?"

James nodded and waved me off.

I was heading out of the reception hall when Elly, dressed in a sexy but modest floor length evening gown, came rushing towards me. "Rio! Thank God you guys are here. I need to attend the ceremony but I'll be back before the other guests get in. Do you need anything?"

I put my hands on Elly's shoulders and gave them a calming squeeze as I stared into her frightened green eyes. "We've got things handled here. Breathe and relax. You're going to be okay."

She nodded slowly and took a couple of deep breaths before I let her go. "Thanks," she said with a soft smile. "I'm so glad you guys are here." She rapidly blinked back some tears before steeling herself.

Stacy

Valet parking was free so I let them take my ancient Honda Civic for a drive as I stepped up the expansive marble stairs leading to the open door of the very well maintained historical plantation home. I should have been surprised that Jen would want to get married in a place like this, but I wasn't. It was actually very fitting that she would get married in the place where rich people used to live and rule over others. It wouldn't surprise me in the least if these were her ancestors. Could she really be blamed for having meanness in her blood?

Yes, probably she could.

The air was awash with the smell of brand-new taffeta and hundreds of blooming peonies. There was a grand staircase straight ahead that met midway with two staircases that cascaded down on either side of the upper floor. As I entered I was handed a program and a glass of champagne. Perhaps this wedding wouldn't be so bad after all.

I was ushered along with my drink and program in hand to the right which led down a short hallway into a large room and out into the side yard of the large plantation house. I pulled my coat tightly around me as I made my way under the outdoor tent that was set up for the ceremony. When I reached my seat on the groom's side I sat down and removed my coat. It was surprisingly warm in the tent.

I looked around to see if there was anyone I knew, but I couldn't recognize any familiar faces. I sighed softly as I turned around. I opened my program and looked it over slowly, biding my time until Elly arrived. Just before the music started up Elly came over and sat down next to me.

"Thanks for saving a seat," she whispered.

"I was wondering if you were going to make it. You doing okay?" I searched her face quickly before she turned it away from me with the starting notes of the wedding processional music. She didn't look alright. She looked sad, defeated, torn... Miserable. I shoved my glass of champagne towards her and she quickly gulped it down before handing the empty glass back to me.

Everyone stood.

I inhaled deeply as I turned my eyes, as was customary and polite, towards Jen as she started her walk down the aisle. As she walked in and my eyes followed her all I could think about was Elly and how much pain she must be in knowing that this woman was about to take the life Elly wanted for herself.

I looked at Kent over my shoulder and saw him staring at Elly. His eyes darted back to Jen when our eyes clashed. I hope he saw the anger in mine. He was making a mistake and subconsciously, at least, he knew it.

After Jen was at the altar the guests sat and listened. All except for me. I was too busy looking at Elly, wondering if she was going to be able to hold it together. Wondering how she could be so strong at a moment like this when the man she loved so much was getting married to another woman.

"Are you okay?" I whispered into her ear.

She nodded but kept her glassy eyes staring straight ahead.

I went to reach for her hand but she slunk out of her seat at the same moment. I watched as she walked down the aisle, hunching her shoulders, trying to pretend as if she were invisible. But she was very much visible. People started to turn around when the groom's eyes fell on her retreating backside.

I shook my head as I turned around in my seat and waited for the torture that was this ceremony to end. While sitting there I had a moment to reflect on my previous evening with Jordan. The date had been nice. But that was all. Just nice. Jordan was everything I should have wanted and yet the whole time I was thinking about Rio. What would Rio have done when the waiter brought me the wrong order? Would he have made me wait the fifteen minutes until the waiter came back to fix the problem because he didn't want to cause extra trouble? What would Rio have done when a group of guys catcalled me from the side alley?

It was exhausting wondering all night what Rio would have done differently. I only had to remind myself that Rio would have done what Chance would've. He would've told me to quit bitching and eat the damn dinner. He would've grabbed my ass and tried to slip his finger under my skirt to show that he was the top dog with a woman as fine as me. That's what Chance would've done. And Rio and Chance were cut from the same cloth. I'd already dated a Rio and it hadn't turned out well at all. Despite how much my heart told me I wanted to do it again my mind knew that I had to stay away. I'd seen that movie already. It didn't have a happy ending.

Chapter 6

Rio

As we finished fine tuning, Elly came back into the large ballroom. The guys looked at me for some sort of direction. I shook my head and looked at the scuffed up black collapsible stage blocks beneath my feet.

"Are you guys ready?" she asked, her voice strained with beaten back emotions.

"Yep," we said in unison.

I cleared my throat and looked at James and Frank, giving them a 'What the fuck is wrong with you? You're going to fuck this up' stare. Frank moved into action first, putting his arm around Elly's shoulder. I closed my eyes tight and swallowed back the wince. I wasn't a woman wizard or anything but I knew enough from the years spent with my mother and sister that you didn't touch a woman or ask her if she was alright. It was an invitation for a tear-stained shirt.

"How are you doing, Elly? Doing okay?"

She let out a phony giggle and slid out from under his arm. "I'm fine. I'm fine, you guys," she reiterated after glancing between all of us. "He's getting married to her. She is going to make him happy and that's what matters." She swallowed hard and it was obvious she had more to say but she couldn't get it out. "I'll be right back."

She left us staring at her back and then each other.

"Well, there goes all our future wedding gigs," James said, joking.

"I hope she's alright," Frank said, pulling idly on his earlobe. I hoped so too or this was going to be one hell of a wedding performance.

Just before the guests started flowing into the ballroom, Elly came back on stage. She was poised and confident, her shoulders back and her head high. But when she looked at me I saw it. The sadness. The hurt. The pain.

"Here goes nothing," she said with a small smile.

I nodded and took my place to her right, Frank to the left. And our first wedding gig commenced.

As people started to usher in I tried to look at their faces. There wasn't much to look at, per se, just a sea of unfamiliar people. Elly was mid-lyric when I spotted Stacy's red hair pulled back into a tidy up-do leaving her long slender neck exposed. Her dark blue dress shimmered above her black tights as she walked towards the seating chart.

My finger fumbled on the strings. I cursed quietly and I was probably the only one who noticed that she'd fucked up my concentration. I glanced out again, searching for her. Our eyes clashed, a tightness spurned in my gut. She waved her fingers in my direction and I nodded.

I played on and kept pace as I watched her cross the large room. Watching her now I felt like I was seeing the real Stacy, not the one who pretended she was fast and loose. This Stacy was elegant and put together. She had control of herself and her life. She looked pretty damn appealing from up here on the stage. And then she went to the bar and my interest almost instantly sizzled out.

That's why it wouldn't work, I had to remind myself. She was a drinker. She wouldn't understand that she'd have to give it up to be with me. Fuck, I was getting ahead of myself. I didn't want to be with her. I couldn't. I would just fuck up her life by getting her deep into my shit after asking her to change herself for me. How fucking selfish would that be?

As we moved through the set list I'd occasionally sneak a glance at Stacy. She always seemed to have a drink in her hand. But much to my secret pleasure she was almost always alone. She wasn't hanging on a man. I'd even caught her staring at me a few times.

Elly took a break and we switched over to some jazzy pre-recorded stuff. I set down my bass and found my feet taking me towards Stacy as the rest of the band went outside to take a breather. I stopped at her table, my hands shoved into my pockets. I cleared my throat and once her beautiful eyes were staring up at me I spoke. "Mind if I have this dance?"

The myriad of strangers around the table were smiling in our direction. Stacy glanced around to see if anyone would protest on her behalf. No one did. "Um, sure." She grabbed her napkin and set it on her seat as she stood up. With heels we were just about eye to eye.

She held onto the crook of my arm as I guided us towards the dance floor. I was hesitant to touch her because I knew it would set off the sparks that raged between us, but I was also craving them. I wanted to hold her and I knew it was bad for me to want that. "You look nice," I said, my eyes dropping to her dress briefly. It was a modest one but she wore it beautifully.

"Thanks. You look…" she bit her lower lip gently, her eyes raking over my chest. "Fucking hot in a tux."

I chuckled and felt warmth bubbling in my chest at her compliment. "Thanks.

Are you enjoying yourself?"

"Um, no. I don't know any of these people. Except for Kent and he's the groom and extremely busy dancing and getting to know his new extended family. How about you? Are you enjoying yourself?"

"I am now." I swallowed hard after I'd said it. I shouldn't have said that. I was going to give her the wrong idea. Fuck, what was wrong with me?

She smiled softly and dropped her eyes to my mouth. "You're quite the charmer when you want to be, Rio." I felt the heat of her body against mine as she moved in closer, her arms tightening around the back of my neck. We moved together more slowly. It was torture holding her in my arms. Her scent surrounded me, drowning my thinking brain. My eyes dropped to her luscious lips that shimmered just like her dress.

"I've never heard that before." She moaned softly and it was nearly my undoing. I looked away, desperate for a distraction and I found one. I spotted Elly coming back into the room. "Thanks for the dance. Time to go back," I said, my smile now gone as I gently pushed Stacy away from my body.

Elly looked different now. Somber. Crushed. I was confused and wondered what had happened in the last fifteen minutes. Had someone hurt her? The fucking groom? Someone else? I approached with clenched fists, ready to protect her, feeling that brotherly instinct kicking in. Our eyes met and she smiled through the hurt.

"Where is the band?"

"Outside. I'll go get them."

Stacy

I had to get out of there. The near kiss with Rio had left me weak in the knees, weak in my resolve. If I didn't stay far away from him I was going to grab onto his sexy tux jacket and beg him to bury himself inside me in front of all of those rich people even though I knew he was no good for me.

I inhaled the fresh, cool night air. I let it relieve me of the heat I'd collected as I'd danced close to Rio. Rio. I closed my eyes and inhaled deeply again. I shouldn't have agreed to come. I knew this was going to be trouble. I heard the shuffle of shoes in the grass behind me and when I turned I saw a tall, muscular dark haired man with tortured dark eyes. Kent. He looked more off than usual.

He waved to me and then shoved his hands in his pockets and turned his face to the moon. He closed his eyes and did the same deep breathing techniques that I'd been doing myself so I knew he must have been having some inner turmoil himself.

"Do you regret it?" I asked, my words slightly slurred to my own ears. Rio had gotten me completely off-balance.

He raised his eyebrows and looked at me. "Hmm?"

"Do you regret it?" I repeated, slightly louder after clearing my throat.

"Mmm." He glanced down at his arm and pulled his sleeve back, a fresh tattoo staring back at him. I'd seen the same thing on Elly's wrist. I frowned as I stared at him again. His eyes softened and he shook his head, pulling his sleeve back down. He stared at the moon again. "She's too good for me."

I didn't ask who she was. I knew. He'd meant Elly. I looked at the moon with him, letting silence pass between us. He was right. She was too good for him. He didn't deserve her. Not after all the hell he'd put her through.

"Kent? Are you out here?" An older female's voice rang out through the grass. Kent's chest rose and fell heavily.

"Yeah Mom, I'm here." He glanced at me and offered me a tilted half smile. "Gotta get back. Bye Stacy. Thanks for coming."

"Bye," I said as I watched him retreat back towards the punishment he'd doled onto himself.

"Last dance, Kent. What were you doing out here?" I heard his mother say as she wrapped her arm around his and walked with him back inside.

"Just needed some air, Mom."

I stayed outside, letting the cool air comfort me. I groaned as I pushed my hair back from my face. I listened, really listened, and heard the chirping crickets, the cars passing by on a road out of sight and the band playing. Elly's soothing voice was telling me that we were both going to get through it all. I waited until the song ended and the cheers of people seeing the bride and groom off to fade before I headed back into the building.

They were breaking down their instruments, all the guys had stripped their jackets off. Elly was helping as best she could. I staggered over and sat down on the stage and looked up at them. Except Rio, I avoided his gaze.

"Do you guys need any help?"

Elly's eyes searched my face. She grinned and shook her head but I could see that she'd been crying. I tugged on Elly's dress and then held my arms out to her. Her face crumpled and she stepped down and let me hold her. She cried against my shoulder. My eyes met with Rio's and he shook his head before turning away. I wondered if he'd ever experienced that kind of love. The kind of love that could tear you apart and make it near impossible to put the pieces back together again.

I rubbed her back. "Let's get you home, Elly."

Elly pulled away and wiped at her eyes as she turned away from the band and walked towards the exit. Just before she reached the door Jen's mother stopped her.

"Elly! You and the band were amazing!" She pressed something into Elly's hands and then patted them. "Are you alright, dear?"

Elly nodded and I spoke up, "She's just so happy for Kent and Jen. Weddings, right?" She smiled and then pulled Elly away.

When we were in my car she opened her hand and looked at the large wad of hundred dollar bills that lay there. She clasped the bills tightly into her hand as her head lowered towards her knees. My heart ached for her as she let out a strangled sob. I put my hand on her shoulder and gave it a squeeze. There was nothing I could say to take away her pain so I didn't even try. I rubbed and waited until she'd gotten out what she needed to.

I was familiar with this situation. My mother had been bent over the kitchen table crying her eyes out one too many times because of the string of men she chose to bring home and let into her heart.

And much like then I was now with Elly, while muttering soft words meant to let her know that I was here for her. That someone was here despite the fact that her heart had just been crushed into a billion tiny pieces.

"I'm sorry," she sniffled as she wiped at her eyes, fortifying her resolve.

"It's fine, Elly. Take your time."

"Let's go home," she said. It was music to my ears.

Chapter 7

Rio

All I could think of the day following the wedding were the two women who had infiltrated my life a week ago. Stacy because she was Stacy and I wanted her. Elly because she'd been absolutely crushed the last time I'd seen her. The problem was aside from band practice I had no real reason to reach out to her. I could reach out just because but it might seem strange considering we were still casual acquaintances.

"Hey man, when are we getting paid for the gig last night?" James asked as he came over to sit beside me during our lunch break, a huge meatball sub in his hands.

I couldn't help but smile. He'd just offered me the perfect reason to track Elly down and possibly Stacy too, if Elly was M.I.A. "I don't know, man."

"Well, fucking call her." He took a large bite of his sandwich as he stared at me.

"Alright, Jesus." I dialed her number and waited. It took a few rings but finally there was an answer.

"Hello?"

I frowned as the voice pass through my brain. That didn't sound like Elly. That sounded like...Stacy. I pulled the phone from my ear to check the number I'd dialed. No, it was definitely Elly's number.

"Stacy?"

"Yeah. Why are you calling Elly? Band business? Because I've gotta tell you, that's not really a priority for her right now."

"Um, no," I rubbed the back of my head. How did she know I was calling about band business? I'm such a fucking idiot. "I was just calling to check up on her. She looked like she was in really bad shape last night when you guys left."

There was a pause on the other end of the line. "Wow. Well, I'll let her know that you called."

"Is she going to be okay? Do you have to go to work or something? I could come over and keep her company."

"I'm calling out. She'll be fine. She just needs time to get over it."

"Or she might never get over it." I cleared my throat after that seeped between us. "Is there anything I can do?" I ran my fingers over my hair as I pushed away from the table and started pacing.

"There might be. What are you doing right now?"

"Uh," I hadn't expected her to actually be interested in anything that I had to offer, now or ever. "I'm on my lunch break."

"That's cool. Look, call back after you're done at work and I'll let you know if there is anything you can do for her."

"Okay, great, thanks."

With finality the line went dead. I shoved it into my pocket and went back to the table. James was staring at me. "What?"

"You didn't even ask her."

"She's not feeling good, man, cut her a break."

He scoffed as he crumpled up the wrapper from his sub and pushed away from the table. "I can't believe she's lovesick over that tool. It's going to be up to us to help her forget all about him."

"Well, it won't be all on us, but yeah, if she stays in the band we're going to have to take her under our wing."

He threw his trash away and then came back, hands on the top of the chair he was standing behind. "Speaking of taking people under our wings... how are you doing?"

I glanced up and nodded. "I'm good. Thanks."

"Oh, right," James said, pointing at me with both fingers. "Moms wanted to know if you're coming over for dinner tomorrow night."

"Pot roast night?" James nodded. "Hell yes. I will be there." James nodded once more, with finality and then headed for the door.

"Cool. Later, tater!"

***

I took my phone out and was about to dial Stacy's number but then thought better of it.

RIO: WHAT IS ELLY'S ADDRESS?
STACY: WHY?

RIO: I WANT TO SEND HER SOMETHING.
STACY: WHAT DO YOU WANT TO SEND HER?
RIO: IT'S PERSONAL.
STACY: IS IT GOING TO UPSET HER?
RIO: I SURE AS SHIT HOPE NOT. WHAT'S HER ADDRESS?

It was a few minutes before she responded and finally gave up the address.

STACY: IF IT UPSETS HER I'M GOING TO KICK YOUR ASS.

I smirked as I headed into the best pizza shop in town. Ten minutes later I was driving towards Elly's apartment, the pizza strapped to the back of my motorcycle. Riding on a bike was just enough of a thrill to satisfy me. I didn't drive like an asshole but there was something freeing about being exposed to all the elements, feeling the wind through my hair, feeling the sun beat down on my body.

I arrived at Elly's apartment and knocked on the door, pizza in hand. I was standing out there for a few minutes before the door finally opened. Stacy was there, looking more like the morning after we'd slept together in a tank top and a pair of oversized sweatpants. It stirred up memories for me and I struggled to keep my dick from stirring in my pants. It was fucked up because the morning after we hadn't fucked, she'd just left me in bed like a chump. Which I was.

"Hey. I thought you girls could use some sustenance."

Her eyes moved over my body so I took the liberty of looking over her body too. She was gorgeous. I cleared my throat to get her attention so that my thoughts didn't go to places they really shouldn't be going. She took in my raised eyebrows and I saw the blush creep over her cheeks.

"Thanks." She held her hand out for the pizza.

I scoffed, "You're not going to throw me out into the street after I've brought you dinner, are you? I'm hungry too. I was hoping to share."

She rolled her eyes and stepped back to let me in. I entered and my eyes briefly wandered over the space. There were tissues stacked impressively high on the coffee table. I wondered if they could even see the screen when they were sitting on the couch. Elly came out of the bathroom. She looked depressing as hell. Her nose was red, her eyes were puffy, and her hair looked like a bunch of mice had started nesting in it.

I turned away before she caught any sort of pity in my expression and headed for the kitchen, the pizza starting to hurt my hand from the heat it was emitting. I put slices on plates and then took two and brought them out to the living room.

The girls had been whispering to each other and it stopped the instant I was headed their way.

"Don't stop on my account," I said with a grin. I held a plate out for each of them and they took it in stride. "What are we watching?" I glanced at the TV briefly.

"Sense and Sensibility," Elly said with a sniffle as she settled herself into the couch, looking as if she wanted to sink into it so much to make herself disappear.

"Awesome. Haven't seen that one but I'm sure I'll love it."

"I don't remember anyone inviting you to stay," Stacy snapped, still standing, ready to face off with me.

I grinned at her spunk. I loved it. I looked at Elly, "Can I stay and watch?"

She shrugged her shoulders as Stacy sighed and sat down on the couch with a huff. She was mumbling to herself as she crossed her legs and shoved her pizza towards her mouth.

I nabbed my pizza and went back to the living room, sitting right between Elly and Stacy. As far as things went, I was in a pretty good position. I glanced at both of them, flashing them my charming grin. Neither fell for it. Tough crowd.

I shrugged it off as I devoured my pizza and got lost in a movie about a time long ago where manners and appearances were king.

Stacy

For the hundredth time Rio's elbow grazed my arm and I felt the familiar prickles of anticipation for something that wasn't going to come. I wondered if he felt the same sensations or if he's doing it because he knew it was making me uncomfortable. I wouldn't put it past him to do something so cruel. He was a bad boy, after all.

I couldn't believe he'd showed up at my apartment. He hadn't known it was my address when I'd given it to him and I sure wasn't about to divulge that information now. It was best he thought it was Elly's place. The last thing I'd need is for him to show up at my door uninvited.

I tried to ignore the feeling of loss when he stood up with Elly.

"I'm going to take a shower, guys. Thanks for the pizza, Rio. I'll see you at band practice in a couple of days."

Rio nodded to Elly. "Sure thing. Oh, um..." He scratched the back of his neck nervously. "James was wondering when he was going to be paid for the gig."

I whipped around and glared at Rio. "Are you serious right now?"

Elly held her hand up to silence me. "It's fine. I have it. Hold on." She went to her purse and pulled out the large wad of cash and held it out to Rio. "Here you go. Just pay me my share the next time I see you."

"But!-" I interjected again. I didn't want her to leave me alone with Rio. Who knew what would happen.

"Stacy, it's fine. I'll be out in a minute." Without another word Elly disappeared into the bathroom.

I tried to avoid looking at Rio, I looked everywhere but at him. "So, I guess you're going to go now?"

He shoved the wad of cash into his jeans pocket. "Yeah, I probably should," he said, his voice thick as he stared at me. When I didn't say anything he nodded. "Okay." He grabbed up the dirty dishes and brought them to the sink despite my protest. "Look, I..." he paused, his hands on the counter as his eyes roamed freely over my body, sending shivers of delight through me. He shook his head. Whatever he'd been about to say was forever gone. "If you need anything you know how to reach me."

"Yeah." I moved towards the door with his leather jacket in my hands and he met me there. Our fingers touched briefly as the jacket exchanged hands. The sexual tension between us was literally sparking.

"Thanks," he said, his blue eyes as electrically charged as my body. His slow, easy grin lit up the rest of his face and my nerves.

"Sure." I had to do something to make the feelings I was having for him go away or I'd be drowning in them. I needed to dump some ice on his feelings and harden his heart towards me. I wouldn't have the will-power to resist him if he wanted to touch me again. "Goodnight."

I let out a breath I hadn't known I was holding as I watched the door close behind him.

When I was finished cleaning up the dishes Elly came out from the shower, wrapped in a towel.

"Hey. How are you feeling?"

"Like I'm ready to be done crying. I want to go out and get really, really drunk."

I stripped the gloves from my fingers and set them on the counter. "Are you serious right now?"

She stared at me, dead on. "Like a heart attack."

"Okay," I said, nodding my head. "Let's get you fucking drunk! Do you want to stay in or go out?"

"Go out. I want to get prettied up and make some more bad choices. You only live once, right?"

I nodded again. My mind immediately on Rio and the bad choice he'd be and how much I wanted to make that bad choice all over again.

No, Stacy! You need to make good choices now. Stay on track.

"Right. You only live once and tonight if you want to get really drunk and kiss a stranger then you should do that! And I'll watch you make all the bad choices for a change."

"Deal." She sauntered over to my closet. "Now, what to wear..."

Chapter 8

Rio

I opened my fridge and stared at the almost vast emptiness. I needed to go to the grocery store but I wasn't in the fucking mood. I shut the fridge roughly and pulled my phone out, dialing James.

"Yo! What's up?" His voice was familiar and worked only a little at calming my nerves.

"What are you doing?"

There was a slight pause before he responded, "I'm just sitting on my couch, my hand in my pants."

I had no doubt that was exactly what he was doing.

"You wanna go out? I have your cut from the gig."

"Fuck yes! Where you wanna go?"

"Slick Willy's," I said only because I knew it was his favorite place. The place where the half-dressed waitresses danced on the bars, flashing their ass cheeks each time they turned in their daisy duke cutoff shorts.

"Fuck. Yes. I'll meet you there in thirty."

***

It was loud and crowded because it was a Saturday night. I snagged a couple of seats in the middle of the bar when a couple abandoned them to go to the dance floor. When I glanced over my shoulder again I saw James coming towards me, a huge-ass grin on his face. He clapped me on the shoulder as he sat down.

"I'm in heaven!" He glanced at the bartender whose tits were barely concealed and ordered himself a beer.

"Coke." I wasn't going to break my sobriety because I was sulking over Stacy. I just needed to be surrounded by people, drunk or not. Maybe I could find someone else to distract me. I glanced around while we waited for the bartender to get our drinks. Maybe not. No one in the place looked even remotely appealing.

"So, dude. What happened? Some shitty thing happen at work?"

I grabbed my Coke and took a sip, swallowing back the fizzy liquid as I tried to figure out what I was going to say to James who was staring at me.

"No. I just wanted to get out of the house."

James and I regarded each other and he finally shook his head. "No, that's not it. Woman troubles?"

I took another large gulp, almost choking myself. I looked around for a distraction, anything. I pointed at a lady who seemed to be all alone on the far end of the bar. "I bet you can't get her number."

James looked briefly before turning back to me. "Nice try. Do you know whose number I want?" I waited for him to answer his rhetorical question as he took a long pull from his beer. "Stacy."

My jaw clenched involuntarily as I stared into my Coke. It took me a second to bite back everything my stupid caveman mind wanted to say to my friend and when all that crazy shit passed I answered him. "She's dating someone."

"Damn. Sucks for me." He glanced around and then turned all the way around on his stool, his arms taking over the space of the bar as his eyes locked onto someone. "Damn..."

I turned my head to see who he was staring at and I found myself staring at Stacy, dressed in a tied up plaid shirt and a pair of skin tight jeans. She turned in the middle of the dance floor and started to line dance.

"I didn't expect to see her out and about."

Absently I responded, "Stacy?" I couldn't peel my eyes away from her. Everything inside of me wanted to get up and go to her. I wanted to be behind her, my hands on her hips. I wanted to smell her hair. Fuck, I had it bad. I was obsessing over her more than I had been about alcohol. I guess that counted for something.

He snickered, pulling me from my thoughts. "No, Elly. You did call and check on her after work, didn't you?"

I blinked and looked around again; Elly was dancing next to Stacy. It irked me that I hadn't seen her right away. I had blinders on. Stacy blinders. I was fucking losing it. I gulped back my Coke and set my empty glass on the bar.

"Yeah, I stopped by. I'm surprised she's out. I thought she was going to sleep it off."

"Maybe Stacy told her to quit fucking whining and get back into bed. With a stallion." I gave James a warning look. He snickered again and held his hands up innocently. "Dude, I was joking. She's in the band. I wouldn't fuck the band over like that. I'm not a total douchebag."

"You learned your lesson, you mean. Katie was a great singer."

"And a total psycho," James countered.

I shrugged it off. "Maybe we should bring them a couple of beers."

He pointed his beer bottle in their direction. "Or maybe those dudes trying to get them to dance will do it."

I was up and out of my chair before I even know what I was doing. A tall guy with a cowboy hat was about to pull Stacy into a dance when I put my hand on his shoulder to stop him.

"Mind if I have this dance?" I looked right at her, ignoring the guy altogether.

She blushed and shrugged, looking at the stranger with apologetic eyes. There was some satisfaction as I pulled her into my arms and started to dance with her. I could tell by the look on her face that she wasn't expecting me to know the steps. I'd spent many a drunken night on a dance floor much like this one. I twirled and two-stepped around with her on the dance floor to music that made my ears want to bleed. It was worth it to hold her in my arms.

"You're pretty good," she said loudly to be heard above the music.

I smirked, "You're not bad yourself." I upped my game as the tempo increased. A few spins and she was laughing. I forgot myself and my promise to my sponsor and as the song ended I pulled her against me and brought my lips to hers.

Stacy

Oh this was good. But bad. So bad. I pushed him away and frowned up at him. "I told you I'm seeing someone."

"I don't see him here, do you?"

I glanced over his shoulder and my eyes met with Jordan's face. "Actually, I do."

Rio turned his head to look. "Really? That fucking guy?"

I looked back to him and shrugged. "Thanks for warming me up." I patted his chest and then stepped around him, leaving him cold on the dance floor. It was cruel but necessary. I hadn't thought that Jordan would show after I'd texted him where we were going to be but I was glad that he was here.

"Hey. You're here!" I grinned even as I hugged him awkwardly and he hugged me back.

"I'm here. Let's get some beers. I need a couple before I'm loose enough to try to impress you like that guy just did."

"Pft. Just a friend of a friend. Not my type," I lied smoothly as I held his hand and walked with him to the bar. Elly was there, chatting with James who was handing her a fresh beer. I kept a tally on Elly's beer count. I didn't want her to accidentally kill herself trying to drink her sorrows away.

"Elly, James, this is Jordan. My date. Jordan, this is Elly, my best friend and the drummer from her band, James."

Jordan shook both their hands with a nod. "Nice to meet you," he replied and then leaned towards the bartender, ordering two beers. I turned to glance around and bumped right into Rio. He grabbed onto my shoulders to keep me from falling backwards in my surprise. His touch sent jolts through me, much to my disappointment.

"Woah there."

I shrugged his hands off and moved closer to Jordan, wrapping my arm around his waist. He loosely wrapped his arm around me too. I looked at Rio, silently telling him to back off. His jaw was clenching tightly under his skin. He turned his attention to Elly.

"How are you feeling, kid?"

She shrugged as she sipped her beer. "I'll be better after a few of these. Why aren't you drinking?"

I pretended not to care when he leaned over and whispered something to Elly.

"Oh. Wow! You probably shouldn't be here then. I mean...doesn't this tempt you?"

He shook his head and his gaze met mine. "Not nearly as much as other things." I felt my heart hammering in my chest and forced my gaze away from his. Why did he have to be so damn charming?

"Good for you," Elly said before downing the rest of her beer.

Jordan handed me a beer and then tapped his against mine. "Cheers," he said with a smile.

"Cheers," I smiled back and then took a long pull. I grabbed his hand and pulled him towards the dance floor when a slow song started. I was proud that I didn't look over my shoulder as I rested my arms on his shoulders. His beer was cold and pressed slightly against the skin that was exposed on my back.

"I was surprised that you texted," he said as he stared down at me.

"Why?"

"I didn't think you had that great of a time with me."

"You'd be surprised about the things that I think," I said, my mind wandering after I said it to Rio as my eyes fell on him. He had his back to me. He was running his hand over Elly's hair. The act so intimate that it startled me. Was he going to go after Elly tonight?

I looked away and smiled at Jordan. That was ridiculous. He wouldn't do such a thing. Would he? I glanced back he was hunched over, talking into her ear while James looked on, a little smirk on his lips.

Oh my god, were they tag teaming her? I closed my eyes and pushed out of Jordan's grasp as a memory I'd long ago banished from my brain came rushing back.

Darkness and male laughter. The sound of zippers and excruciating pain.

"I'm sorry. I have to pee." I put my hand to my head as I made my way towards where Elly was sitting. I grabbed her hand and pulled her with me towards the bathroom. Once we were inside the dark and dusky room I blinked at her, tears filling my eyes for reasons I didn't want to think about.

"Are you okay? Was he hitting on you?"

Elly looked confused and she shook her head. "What? Who?"

"James and Rio. Were they hitting on you?"

"Um... no. At least I don't think so." Her eyes roamed over me, exposing me. "Are you okay?"

I downed the rest of my beer and then threw the bottle into the trashcan. "Yeah, I'm fine. I just wanted to make sure you were okay. It looked like they were wolves ready to pounce and devour you."

She looked shocked. "Stacy you slept with him, I would never do that. And besides he's way too cool for me. He's not my type. I'm not interested in him. At all. And I'm pretty sure the only one here who he is interested in is you. And as for James, well, he's just... crazy. Hot to look at but once he opens his mouth." She shook her head, the look of disgust on her face made me realize I had misjudged the situation.

I scoffed, "Okay, I'll be watching and if you feel like you're in trouble you just give me a signal."

"Okay, like what?"

"Something like, 'HELP!'"

For the first time since the wedding I saw her smile.

Chapter 9

Rio

The two of them had come out of the bathroom and headed immediately for the dance floor. Stacy paused as her eyes fixated on someone. I turned to see who it was and the frown on my face probably said it all. Jordan, her date or boyfriend or whatever the fuck he was, was dancing with another girl, their bodies grinding in ways that should have been reserved for a private room. Why he would do that, I had not the faintest idea. Fucking idiot.

I quickly grabbed James by the shoulder and pulled him towards Elly and Stacy who had stopped by an abandoned table littered with crushed cigarette butts and empty beer bottles.

"Hey, let's get out of here. I'm the designated driver, where do you want to go?"

Stacy was still staring at Jordan, her face emotionless. Elly looked between us before finally speaking up, "I'm kind of hungry."

I nodded as my eyes met with Stacy's. She looked like a mixture of anger and disappointment. Had that guy really meant that much to her? I glanced over my shoulder to Jordan. How dare he hurt Stacy's feelings? I was going to hurt his face. I took a step towards the dance floor but I was stopped by a warm hand on my wrist pulling me back.

"Don't. If I wanted someone to punch him I'd do it myself. Let's go."

I followed after James who had wrapped an arm around Elly's waist and led her towards the exit. We all piled into Stacy's little car and as we started to drive Elly started to moan from the back seat.

"Oh god, she's going to puke!" James had leaned forward and was yelling directly into my ear, causing the car to swerve a little. "Dude, that's not going to help!"

"Quit fucking yelling at me. Jesus."

My house was the closest and so I took us all there. We climbed out of the car and I carried Elly after handing James the keys to unlock the door. Stacy was following behind. I felt her eyes on me. I wanted to turn around to be sure but Elly's well-being was the most important right now.

I brought her into my bedroom and laid her down on the edge of the bed. I grabbed my bathroom trash can, which luckily I'd emptied earlier, and set it beside the bed. "Puke in here if you need to, Elly."

She groaned again, her eyes shut tight.

There was nothing I could really do for her. Nothing any of us could do except watch her to make sure she didn't choke on her own vomit. I turned around and saw James and Stacy staring at me in the doorway. I rubbed the back of my head in frustration. James came forward, a bottle of water in his hand. "I'll stay on babysitting duty. She'll be okay. She's just going to hurt tomorrow. Go on, you two. Get the hell out of here. Elly and I have some drunken secrets to share." Elly groaned lightly beside him.

Stacy looked at me with disbelieving eyes. I shook my head. "We can trust him. I wouldn't be friends with a complete asshole."

"Love you too, man!" James yelled and then covered his mouth, realizing his volume was too loud.

I closed my bedroom door and then pushed Stacy towards the kitchen so James wouldn't overhear me. "He's an asshole to women he sleeps with, sure, but that's because..." I glanced over my shoulder to the closed door. "He's still recovering from a broken heart, that's all. He's not a bad guy. And he has three little sisters. He knows what he's doing. We have a no fraternizing rule when it comes to the band. He wouldn't risk it."

She still looked at my wearily.

"Do you drink like that all the time? Are you the party girl type?" I asked.

She shrugged her shoulders. "Not all the time."

"Most of the time?"

"Maybe."

I grabbed us both some water and then moved to the kitchen table. She sat across from me. After a couple of gulps I changed direction again.

"The guy you were seeing is kind of a dick."

She froze in place, as if she'd been caught stealing something. I watched as her thoughts churned in her mind, her upper teeth worrying her lower lip as she decided, I presumed, on what to say about it.

"He isn't who I thought he was."

"Ah. Well I guess it's a good thing you didn't purposely seek out dating a dick."

Her eyes collided with mine and I felt something churn in my gut.

"I'm over those kinds of guys. Maybe I'm over guys altogether. I've never found one outside of books and movies that was worth a damn."

"Wow. Daddy issues?"

She looked as if she'd been slapped. I instantly regretted it. Apparently she did have daddy issues. I could relate. Before I could say I was sorry she pointed an angry finger at me.

"See. Case in point."

I scoffed, "I'm not a dick. I'm observant."

"Whatever." She rolled her eyes and then started to peel the label from the bottle of water.

"Look, I didn't mean to offend you but this one guy fits all attitude is bullshit. I would never have let another woman take your place if I had been in his shoes."

"Yeah. Right."

I frowned at her. "What would it take to convince you of that?"

She closed her eyes, defeated, and shook her head, "I don't know, Rio. Time. But I can't–I won't–" She sighed in exasperation. "I'm not going to give you a chance."

"Why the hell not?" Not that I wanted her to give me a chance. Not yet, anyway. I wasn't ready for her and all her drama. But if I was ready then...

"Because... of your bad judgement. You picked me up in a bar and brought me to your house. That speaks to your character. And not very well."

I inhaled and exhaled deeply, annoyed that she drew such hard lines when it came to mistakes.

"Yeah, and what does that say about your character, Stacy? I didn't rape you. I didn't take you here against your will. It takes two to have a one night stand and I wasn't alone in that."

She nodded, clearly not impressed with my debate skills. "That's great. Attack me."

"You started it."

"Listen to yourself. You're acting like a big fucking baby."

"Excuse me for wanting to defend my character. I don't like being judged any more than you do. I'm not some jackass who walks around with a hard on looking for somewhere to stick it. Before you I hadn't had sex with a woman in over two years. And that wasn't because I didn't have any offers. It was because I wasn't interested. And if I hadn't fucked up and been drunk the night we met I probably wouldn't have taken you home either. But I made a fucking mistake and I did. And now you're sitting over there and judging the shit out of me when you did the same goddamn thing."

She was silent for a long moment. "You're right. That's not fair to judge you based solely on that. But there are other things."

"Yeah? Like what?"

Her eyes were going crazy, looking everywhere but at me. And I knew why. She had fucking nothing.

After a long moment she sighed. "Look, it doesn't matter. Everyone can hide who they are for a little while but then the truth comes out. And the truth of it is that deep down every guy is a bad guy. I have never, and I mean never, seen a man who had a good heart underneath."

I shook my head and looked away. "That's the saddest fucking thing I've ever heard."

"Fuck you. I don't want your pity. I don't want anything from you." The chair scraped against the linoleum as she stood up from the table.

"Good. Because I don't have anything to give you, Stacy."

With daggers in her eyes she pushed her hands off the table and spun around. With giant determined steps she walked away towards the front door. When I heard keys jangling I realized her intent and quickly got up to follow her. No way in hell was she going to be driving home drunk. She barely got down the driveway before I wrapped my arms around her waist from behind and picked her up.

"Let me go!" she exploded, her strong legs kicking, trying to throw me off balance.

"Not if you're planning on driving that fucking car," I bellowed, struggling to keep hold of her as my feet slid in the snow that had fallen on the ground.

"I want to go home! Just let me go!"

Stacy

As much as I'd kicked and struggled it was no use. His grip around my middle was tight.

"Stacy, if you want to go home, I'll take you but I'm not letting you drive yourself."

I went limp in his grasp but he didn't loosen up. Did I want to go home? Hell yes. Did I want him to know where I lived? Hell no. Fuck. I was stuck here until I was sober enough to convince this maniac that I could drive myself. Or. . .

"I'll call a cab for me and Elly. Let me go," I said, pushing at his strong forearms locked around my waist. I tried desperately to ignore the feeling of his hard, warm body behind mine.

"Put the keys in my pocket and I'll let you go," he said, his hot breath tickling my neck, sending unwanted shivers through my body.

I reached around and stuffed the keys into his pocket and almost immediately he let me go. When I turned around I saw the anger on his disapproving face. I scowled back. He turned and walked back towards the house, his fists curled by his sides. It wasn't until he was near the top step that I saw that he didn't have any shoes on. Reluctantly I stayed outside and pulled my cellphone from my purse.

I tried four different cab companies before I gave up. There was a major snowstorm coming in and the cabs weren't working until it was safe. I went to my car and leaned against it, not wanting to go in his house, not wanting to see him or his disapproving stare. It had hurt that he was so obviously disinterested in me. Did I have daddy issues? Probably. But it wasn't his place to call me out on it. I just needed to get away and stay away from him. My last semester of school was starting in a couple of weeks and that was where I was going to need to throw my focus anyway. I needed to keep my eye on the prize. The prize, of course, was getting out of the poverty cycle. The prize was not a guy.

No more guys. No more sex. No more. I wished I could have this conversation with Elly. I was sure she'd understand and she would probably even join the pact with me. Her guy had screwed her over big time. I pushed off my car and went back into the house. Just as I opened the door to the bedroom I heard the loud retching of Elly throwing up in the trashcan Rio had set out for her.

I wrinkled my nose and covered my mouth, taking a step back. James was bent over her on the bed, holding her hair back. I stepped back more and shut the door. Nothing made me want to vomit more than smelling vomit. She was going to reek of vomit.

"Rethinking your choices?"

"Shut up or I'll throw up on you."

"Go lay down on the couch." It wasn't a suggestion, it was an order. I would've fought back if I hadn't felt the unwanted burn in the back of my throat. I moved to his living room and laid down on his couch. I put my arms above my head, closed my eyes, and took deep breaths. I could still hear Elly and it was psyching me out.

"TV, please. Music, something," I begged.

I heard his footsteps retreating on the thin carpet and then a cat food commercial jingle. I furrowed my brows and concentrated on the sound of the TV. Slowly I realized that taking Elly anywhere wasn't in the cards. I was going to have to crash here tonight. Or let Rio drive and find out that he already knew where I lived. I wasn't sure I could listen to Elly vomiting all night.

"Rio," my weak voice sounded foreign to my own ears.

"Yeah?" his voice was strained, quiet and close.

I ventured to open my eyes and saw him standing near the TV, his arms crossed over his chest, staring at me. "I can't see the TV."

He glanced over his shoulder and then moved towards the kitchen. "Sorry, Princess."

I was beginning to loathe that nickname. "Well, don't leave!" My eyes followed his form as he paused in the hallway.

"What the hell do you want from me?"

"Um... company? Come watch TV with me."

He pulled some remotes from a drawer before sitting down and then spread himself out the way only a man could.

I scooted to the other end of the couch and glanced at him, his profile was all lines and angles, his arm draped casually over the back of the couch. "Thanks."

He grunted and flipped through the channels on TV. He wiggled in his seat to sink deeper into his leather couch. His focus solely was on the TV and while it was I took the opportunity to study him. He looked comfortable except for his jaw which was still twitching beneath his skin. Was he irritated? I turned towards the TV and crossed my arms over my chest.

I wasn't sure if he was doing it on purpose or not but through his channel surfing the picture stopped on a couple tumbling around on a dark grassy field.

"Oh, yes, Theodore. I will love you forever."

"Even when I'm President, Eleanor?"

"It wouldn't matter to me if you were President or a poor pig farmer, Theodore. I will always be by your side."

I looked at Rio at the same moment he looked me. His face was so serious despite the fact that we were watching presidential soft core porn. I started to cackle and covered it up before it got too loud. He raised an eyebrow at my apparent nuttiness and then started to laugh himself.

He shook his head and flipped the channel. "You're going to make James curious and then he's going to come out here."

"Sorry, sorry." I bent over and removed my heels and then tucked my feet underneath myself. When I glanced over my shoulder again he was staring at me again, his eyes taking in my bare feet and then moving upwards over my jeans which hugged every curve. I felt the heat in my cheeks but instead of looking away I watched as his eyes finally met mine.

I smiled at him but instead of smiling back his jaw clenched again and he looked back to the TV. The disappointment seared me in my gut. And then I was angry at myself for feeling the disappointment. He was just like Chance. I had to stay strong or risk getting my heart broken.

When I glanced at him again, his eyes were still straight ahead, he'd stopped on a movie that had been popular a few years ago. I cleared my throat as I got up and moved away, he glanced up this time as I pointed to the kitchen. "I'm going to get something to drink, do you want anything?"

"Another water would be great. Thanks." He turned back to the TV without another glance.

I smiled to myself as I fetched two of them and then came back. I sat down beside him, and set the water between his legs, causing him to jump from the cold. He grunted and gave me a look of warning. I smiled innocently.

"Sorry." I sipped my water and only half paid attention to the movie as my mind wandered. In less than a year I'd be a college graduate with a degree in Accounting. I'd be living in some awesome apartment filled with suits and grown up furniture. I'd come home to a tall, dark, and handsome man pouring wine to go with the dinner he'd just cooked for me. I'd look up into his gorgeous blue eyes and lean in to kiss him. And then he'd push all the dishes from the table and lay me down on it so he could... I took a big gulp of water as Rio invaded my daydream.

Bad, Stacy. Bad.

I tried to rework the daydream with Josh Grobin in Rio's place but it didn't quite have the same effect. I sighed loudly as I decided to give up the dream all together. No men. Rio glanced over at me, a perplexed expression on his face. "You okay?"

"Yep." I tried to hold back the yawn but I couldn't. "I just need to use the bathroom. I'll be right back." When I came out of the bathroom Rio was busy making up the floor. The couch was already adorned with a pillow and a few blankets.

"So you can sleep on the couch and I'll take the floor," he said.

"No, it's fine. You can sleep on the couch."

I eyed the floor and then looked at him. "Thanks for this," I said as I made my way into the living room. Before I had a chance to sit down he laid down on the floor, hands behind his head.

"I said I was going to sleep on the floor." I glared down at him.

He gazed back. "Yeah. I'm not letting you sleep on the floor. House rules. No women on the floor."

"Hm. That's not a rule I remember you using last time I was here."

I saw a flicker of tension in his jaw as my comment hit the mark. I smiled to myself as I made my way towards the couch and climbed under the blankets. "Goodnight, Rio."

Chapter 10

Rio

It had been hard sleeping on the floor for a number of reasons. Stacy was not ten feet away from me, moaning from time to time in her sleep. Elly was down the hall in my room crying after all the alcohol had violently left her body. And the floor was fucking hard and smelled remotely like cigarettes. I made a mental note to get the damn thing cleaned or replaced. I tossed and turned until dawn peeped through the living room curtains.

I was going to be in a sour mood this morning but there wasn't much I could do to fix that. Coffee would help, but only slightly. I pushed off floor and made my way to the kitchen. I turned on the light over the sink to give me enough to see by but not enough to wake up the moaning Stacy so that I could make some coffee. While it was percolating I went into my bedroom and grabbed myself a shower. Once I was dressed I came back and poured myself a cup of coffee. Coffee in hand I went into the living room to clean up the sad excuse for a bed I'd set up for myself. I growled softly when I heard Stacy mutter my name. "What?" I paused and waited for her to respond. When she didn't I crossed the room and stared down at her. She was sleeping, her cheeks were flushed an inviting shade of pink, and her red hair was a mess of tangles beneath her head. She must have felt my presence because she rolled over and then sleepily opened her eyes. She smiled and I was nearly undone.

"Morning," she murmured and then stretched.

My eyes dropped, watching her body contort and elongate. I sucked in a sharp breath at what I saw. "Be right back." With a loud slam, louder than I'd intended, I put my coffee cup down and went to my room, ignoring for now two of my bandmates who were sleeping.

Damn her and her damn nipples. They were teasing me. I rifled around in my drawers until I found the largest sweatshirt I owned. After a few more minutes of searching I returned to the living room and held out an outfit that could in no way be viewed as sexy.

She eyed the t-shirt, sweatshirt, and basketball shorts with suspicion as she sat up, sleep still heavy on her face. "What's that for?"

"For you. To wear."

"Oh. Um... okay."

My frustration was mounting, her nipples still staring at me, mocking me. I ran a hand through my hair and gave it a tug as I forced my eyes away. "I need to go to the corner store to get some shit."

"You could just stay here and I can go. It's the least I can do for letting us barge in on your life."

"No. I'll go. You're not even in decent clothes."

She looked over her outfit before turning her eyes back to me. "Fine. Go." She snatched up the clothes I'd brought out for her to wear and then disappeared into the bathroom.

I blew out a rough breath when I was finally alone. She was already killing me and she hadn't even been awake for fifteen minutes.

***

"It's really coming down out there," I said as I entered the house with six bags of groceries hanging off my nearly-frozen fingers. Stacy came from the living room where James and Elly were still sitting, and watching TV, and she started to unpack things.

I went back to the door and stripped off my boots and outerwear before padding back, eyeing Elly and James on the way to try to get them to help unload and put things away. "Don't get up. We got it." They didn't even acknowledge me. "I wasn't really sure what you wanted to eat so I got a little of everything," I said. We both reached for the same bag and just as our skin touched she withdrew, grabbing some things and putting them in the fridge. Apparently she was giving me the silent treatment.

That was fine with me. I was putting a jar of peanut butter away when she grabbed the bananas and stuffed them into the fridge. It was then that I remembered the other thing I'd bought, out of impulse, just to be safe, because you never knew what might happen.

I rushed to the bags on the table but Stacy got to it first. She pulled out a box of condoms and held them up with a disapproving stare aimed right at me.

"Really?"

"I was out." I shrugged and pretended I was reaching for the Oreos all along as I grabbed them and put them away in the cupboard.

"And now seemed like a good time to stock up?"

"They were on sale." I took them from her and moved towards my bedroom. It wasn't like I actually thought we were going to roll around in bed together, I was under strict orders to avoid her and a relationship at all costs. And besides, James and Elly were here. They were going to make excellent cock-blockers. But if something did happen again, I wanted to be protected. I didn't need to get a woman knocked up, especially Stacy. I wouldn't want her to be stuck with me for the rest of her life.

I came back out and saw Stacy searching through all the cupboards. I watched for a minute, taking in her shapeless form. Those clothes had been the best decision I'd made since calling my sponsor after my break with sobriety. "What are you looking for?" I asked, trying to be helpful.

"Something to fucking eat," she spit out, like a fluffed up angry kitten.

"Okay. Well, I just got groceries so it shouldn't be too hard to find something. How about a banana?"

"No."

"A bowl of cereal?"

"No."

"An apple?"

"No!" She spun around, her eyes blazing. "I just want some oatmeal. Where is the oatmeal?!"

I held my hands up in defense. "Easy there, Princess." I moved slowly towards the cupboards and reached with slow deliberate movements to get the oatmeal. She snatched it from me and quickly put distance between us.

"Thank you."

I shook my head and moved out of the kitchen to go see what Elly and James were up to. "You guys hungry?" James gaze shot towards me and I held up a hand to keep him from speaking. "Never mind. I know you're hungry. How about you, Elly? Can I make you some pancakes?"

"Carbs?" she asked, her brows furrowed.

"Yes. They're good at helping with hangovers. Do you want some?"

James leaned over and spoke excitedly into her ear. "Say yes, say yes. Please. Please. Please."

Elly covered her ear with a wince and nodded at me. "Pancakes would be great."

I shook my head as I moved back into the kitchen. Stacy was sitting at the table with her bowl of hot oatmeal fresh from the microwave, blowing on it. I had to admit it smelled good. "I'm making pancakes if you want some."

"No, thanks," she said between blows.

I nodded, not sure what else to say. As much as I hated to admit it to myself it was kind of nice having them all here. Before the accident I had been very close to my family. We always ate breakfast and dinner together. We helped cook and clean up afterwards. There were always smiles and laughter. And after the accident all of that changed and there was nothing left but bitterness and blame. My mother had been the one holding us together. She had been our glue.

I glanced out at the winter blizzard currently pummeling my street. Whether I liked it or not we'd be stuck here for at least today. Probably tomorrow as well. I glanced over my shoulder and felt a little disappointment that Stacy was no longer seated there. Despite the arguments we'd had I still wanted her. And I had a sinking feeling as I set the table for three that no matter how sober I became I'd still want her. And that scared the shit out of me. She had been right about one thing. I was no good for her and I needed to stay away.

"Pancakes are ready!"

Stacy

I waited for the three of them to finish up in the kitchen so I could get Elly alone. I wanted to know how she was feeling and I kind of wanted to talk to her about Rio, but I obviously didn't want to do it in front of the other two.

While Rio had been out getting groceries I'd been roaming around his house, cleaning things. Somehow I'd drifted into the garage and I had been so busy thinking about Rio and Jordan and what Jordan's horrible behavior had meant for my plan that I wasn't paying attention and tripped over a cord. There was nothing I could do to prevent the bass guitar from slicing through the front of the bass drum and knocking down the rest of it. When I stood up I regarded the pile of plastic and metal and shook my head. That was going to cost me a pretty penny. I had managed to creep back into the house from the garage without getting caught. I'd fess up to the mess, of course, but I wasn't planning on doing it soon. The blizzard outside was harsh and I didn't want to be given the stink eye and be labeled the girl who fucked up the band's shit until I had somewhere to disappear to.

I stood up and grabbed Elly as James exited the kitchen went down the hallway, scratching his bare stomach. "Thanks for the cakes, dude! They were amazing!" He winked as he passed by me and disappeared into the TV room once more.

I pulled Elly into Rio's room and shut the door behind us. I sat on the bed while she moved towards Rio's nightstand. Four pancakes and a shower had left Elly looking like her old self.

"Feeling better?" I asked.

"Feeling closer to normal," she replied as she picked up her cellphone.

I could tell by the look on her face that Kent had sent her a text message.

"How's Kent doing?"

She closed whatever she'd been staring at and set her phone down as she gathered up the sheets she'd been sleeping on. I got up and grabbed her phone and read the message for myself.

> **I WISH YOU WERE HERE TO SEE THE SUNRISE. IT'S STUNNING.**
> **THINKING OF YOU.**

I laughed. I hadn't meant to but he was utterly ridiculous. "What is wrong with him?" I glanced up at Elly who had started stripping the bed with more force than necessary, her head ducked. She was crying or about to. "I'm sorry, Elly. You've got to tell him what's what, though. You need to set boundaries with him. Especially now that he's married."

"I know. I will when he gets back."

"No," I said, holding the phone out to her. "You'll do it now. Right now. You don't need any more sappy text messages from your married best friend."

She stared at the phone, a few tears leaving her puffy eyes. She let the sheets fall back onto the bed and grabbed the phone. She was furiously typing for a good thirty seconds and then held the phone back towards me.

> **KENT, THAT WAS THE WORST TEXT MESSAGE YOU'VE EVER SENT ME.**
> **SPEND TIME WITH YOUR WIFE AND STOP THINKING ABOUT ME.**

I had to admit I had hoped it would've been a little more beastly than that. I shrugged and turned the phone off, setting it down.

"Is that going to stop him?"

"I don't know. I hope so. I don't want to lose him completely but ..."

"Did you tell him how you felt before he walked down the aisle?"

"No. But..."

"So you want to keep it a secret from him that his marriage is killing you inside because you love him?"

"I don't. I don't love him." She looked angry at me for pressing her. I let her take the sheets away and sat in the middle of Rio's naked bed. I sighed heavily and waited for her to return and when she didn't I began to feel the press of guilt in the middle of my chest. Had I been too hard on her? I got up and was stepping into the hall when my body crashed right into Rio's.

His hands caught my hips and held me steady as my hands grabbed the front of his dark blue pullover sweater. I held my breath and met his eyes which were staring down at me. Surprise quickly turned to desire. I stepped away, smoothing out his sweater where I'd wrinkled it. "Sorry, I was just going to find Elly."

He didn't take his hands off my hips or his eyes off of my face. I felt the blush heating my face, my body responding to the call of his. "She's in the garage with James." He must have seen the flash of concern in my eyes, but before he could question it the garage door opened and slapped against the living room wall loudly.

"MY DRUMS!"

I bit my lower lip and ducked my head, keeping my eyes on Rio because right now he seemed like the less dangerous option. "It was an accident," I said quickly. Rio turned around just as James came angrily striding down the hallway, fire blazing in his eyes. I cowered behind him, my fingers tangling in the back of his sweater for support.

"Dude, chill out. Stacy said it was an accident." Rio held up his hand as James came to a stop in front of him.

"Chill out? I can't replace those! Those are irreplaceable!"

"Dude, they're Pearls. You can get them literally anywhere." Without warning James pulled his hand back and took a swing. Rio stayed right where he was and I gasped as James' fist punched right through Rio's door, narrowly missing his face.

"Fuck!" James pulled his hand out quickly and held it against his chest. It was already bleeding. "I..." A look was exchanged between the two. Some sort of man language that I didn't understand. Rio nodded and then twisted his head towards the left.

James, with a clenched jaw and flaring nostrils, still amped up from his anger, gave a single nod and then made like a thief and exited out the front door.

Slowly Rio let out a loud burst of breath.

"I'll pay for them, of course," I said quietly, stepping out from behind him.

Rio nodded and then rubbed the back of his neck. "I thought he was over her but I guess..." he shook his head. "Someone special to him gave him those drums. We can probably get them fixed up. Don't worry about it. He'll cool down."

I felt terrible. "I think I broke your bass too."

He closed his eyes tight and his shoulders shook once before his lips curled into a tiny smile. He opened his eyes and settled them on me. "It's fine. Replaceable."

I had to admit I was a little relieved. "Where did he go?" I peeked down hallway in time to meet Elly's eyes just before she walked out the front door too. At least she was dressed more appropriately.

"To cool off."

"He might freeze out there."

"He's a big boy, Stacy. He can take care of himself." I followed as Rio moved towards the garage. "When did it happen?" We stepped over the threshold and gasped as I stood next to Rio assessing the damage. I cringed as I looked at the state of James's drums. I'd done quite a number on them.

"This morning after you left to get groceries. I was cleaning and I wasn't paying attention and I tripped over a wire." I crossed my arms under my arms, trying to feel less vulnerable and exposed.

He went over to his bass and picked it up and examined it. The bottom of it was smashed up pretty good. "No one got hurt so that's good."

"Well, James..."

He looked at me and smiled a little. "Yeah, he's a big boy. He can take care of himself."

"Maybe I should go see-" Rio's hand reached out and gripped my arm, holding me in place.

"No, you definitely shouldn't do that." He set his bass down and then led me out of his garage. He locked the door behind us and nodded to the kitchen. "Let's get you nice and distracted so you don't get any crazy ideas."

My brain was already having crazy ideas at his suggestion of distracting me. "Um..."

Chapter 11

Rio

She looked slightly confused when I moved away.

"What kind of distraction?" she asked, her body suddenly in the kitchen too, leaning against my stove.

"A game." I rifled through my junk drawer. I was pretty sure they were in here somewhere.

She shrugged, a mildly disappointed tone in her voice. "It will have to do. We have to find some way to pass the time." I turned to face her, holding up the deck of cards in silent victory.

"War?"

***

"How old were you when you lost your virginity?"

I held back a chuckle. This game of war was starting to get serious. "Sixteen. How about you, Princess?"

She slapped a queen on top of my jack and pulled the pair towards her. "Fourteen."

Fourteen? Fucking Christ. That was the same age my sister had been when–

"Did you love her?"

"Uh..." She interrupted my thoughts and threw me for a loop with that question. What had we been talking about? Right, virginity. "No. I thought I did at the time. Did you love him?"

"I thought I did at the time but he broke my heart." She tossed a two in my direction and I scooped up the small win.

"What's his name? I'll fucking kill him."

She smiled, her eyes twinkling softly as she met my gaze. "Garret Sothers. He's in Boyd County jail. Protected."

"For now," I said with a wink. We both set down a pair of aces and then proceeded to have a war.

"One, two, three. War!"

"Oh, come on!" she shouted as my other ace kicked her king's ass. I grinned as she settled herself back down and we proceeded to play. "Who broke your heart?"

My dad.

I glanced up, her gaze was down on the cards. Thank God I didn't fucking say that out loud. "Britney."

"You don't know her last name?"

"I do. Spears. She fucking broke my heart when she started dating that asshole Justin Timberlake."

The front door slammed shut as James and Elly came back inside effectively cutting off Stacy's laughter. I was a little disturbed that I'd forgotten that they had been out there. No doubt James was near frozen. I swallowed back my unease and stood up from the table as they both entered the kitchen. Stacy looked at me with big, worried eyes. I offered her a smile which seemed to ease her tension a bit. She turned her in her chair, her eyes on James.

"So," James said, looking down at his feet. He looked every bit like a little boy who'd just told his mother to go fuck herself. "I overreacted a little bit and I'm sorry."

"I forgive you, of course. I'm sorry too, for being such a klutz and ruining your drums." She nibbled on her lower lip for a moment before she stood up and extended her arms towards him. I felt jealousy burning in my gut as James arms wrapped around her and pulled her body close to his.

"Okay," he said, ending the hug as quickly as it had begun. He stepped back and glanced between all of us. "There is more good news on top of that apology. The roads have been plowed and we are all free to get out of each other's hair."

I felt the snap of disappointment at the news. Stacy was more fun than I thought she'd be sober and although the sexual tension between us was high we were still able to hold a conversation. Perhaps we could make a go of things once my sobriety was under control and steady. I'd be lying if I said I didn't want to try.

I shoved my hands into my jean pockets and nodded. "Awesome. Let's all get showered and then we can go back to the bar.

"Dibs!" James practically pushed Elly out of the way as he ran towards the bathroom. I sighed heavily.

"We're not going to be getting any hot water, are we?" Stacy asked, crossing her arms over her chest.

I shook my head. "No. Probably not."

Elly shrugged innocently. "I already had one. I'm gonna go watch some TV. Wanna join?"

I looked between the two girls who were staring at each other. Stacy shrugged her shoulders. "Sure." And then they both looked at me.

"Uh, yeah, sure."

***

We watched a whole show before James came out from the bedroom, his hair still damp. He announced there was no more hot water left so we decided to just go to the bar anyway. The ride was longer than usual due to the amount of snowy mush on the road. I noted that Stacy's car had taken a few attempts to finally turn over and get going. I wanted to say something but figured she probably wouldn't appreciate my opinion, so I kept my mouth shut about it.

When we finally arrived at the bar, James and I got out and walked to our vehicles. When the girls left us James came over, hands shoved in his pockets.

"That was cool of you, James, to apologize to Stacy for what happened. I know how much those drums-"

"Yeah. Whatever. Are you coming over for dinner tonight?"

I shook my head at his interruption but ultimately I let it slide. He didn't want to pick at the wound. I got it. "Yeah. I'll be there."

"You gonna be okay?"

I knew he meant was I going to reach for a drink when I was alone. I nodded. I didn't feel any pressure to drink, nothing was wrong in particular. I was solid.

"Cool. I'll see you at dinner then."

As he was walking away my phone rang in my pocket. With hesitation I answered and pressed it to my ear.

"Hello?"

"Hello, Mr. Levant? This is John Ferrell calling from Memorial Hospital. I have Annie Pike here. You are listed as her emergency contact. I'm so sorry that it's taken us so long to get into contact with you but we were finally able to track down your phone number."

My hand clutched the phone tighter. "Annie? What the hell happened to her?"

"She's going to be fine. We treated her and with a little rest, perhaps some rehab, she should be fine."

I scoffed. Annie had been in and out of rehab for as long as I'd known her, which felt like forever but was probably closer to eight years.

"Fine. Is she being discharged tonight?"

"Yes, we've removed what we could and her body took care of the rest. Will you be coming to get her?"

"Yeah, I'm coming."

Annie – it had been at least a year since I'd seen her. I had wondered, of course, what she'd been up to, what kind of company she'd been keeping. I should have been surprised that it wasn't good company, but I wasn't. She had a sordid past and her means of escape was being wholly irresponsible for anything.

She was more of a mess than Elly and Stacy put together and I wasn't particularly happy that she still had my number and that it was only in times like these when she bothered to use it.

It was going to be a long drama filled day.

***

I held Annie's leopard printed purse in my hand as we walked down the quiet, shiny halls to my van. All things considered, she looked pretty good. She still only came up to my shoulder and she looked like she'd been doing less drugs and more eating. Her hair was brown just like my sister's. They used to pretend they were sisters to fuck with people, mostly boys.

"So what's been going on with you?" I asked after we were safely enclosed in the privacy of my van.

She shrugged her slender shoulders, "Nothing, really. Just living. Working, paying bills, partying sometimes."

"Sometimes?" She rolled her eyes at the skepticism in my voice.

"When I'm not working or sleeping. I like to party. So sue me." She pulled a cigarette from her purse and started to light it up.

I yanked it from her lips and held it out to her. "I don't want to smell that shit in my van."

"Touchy." She took it back and shoved it into her purse. She tilted her head back and groaned as I made a sharp turn. Maybe sharper than was necessary. "So what's new with you?"

My first gut reaction was to mention Stacy but instead I snorted. "Nothing. Same job, same house, same band." Annie didn't need to know about my personal business. She didn't really care. She only cared that I was there for her when she needed me and I always would be because I owed it to Penny.

"Same van, same motorcycle. I get it. Same playboy attitude?"

I snorted again. "I wasn't a playboy." It was true that when I was younger I quickly went through the ladies. But I was also drunk off my ass most of the time and being with them was a reason not to be home with my father.

"A heartbreaker? Is that your preferred term?"

"I wasn't a fucking heartbreaker either."

"Please. You were and you fucking know it. Teagan Billows. Hillary Fulston. Essie Gilmore. I can't think of any more names right now, I'm still recovering from death, but I know the list was long."

"I told them exactly what I wanted and they agreed to it."

"It's their fault they thought their love would be enough for you."

My jaw ticked, my frustration mounting. "It's their fault they didn't believe me when I was telling them the truth."

"So no lucky ladies then?"

I wasn't going to tell her shit about Stacy. There wasn't even really anything to tell. We weren't doing anything. We'd just slept together that once. And we wouldn't be doing anything until I was very sober and ready to handle things without my alcoholic crutch. "Nope. Any lucky men for you?"

"Don't you think if I had one I would've put him down as my emergency contact in my phone?"

I grunted noncommittally. "I think every woman I know is single. Except for Maggie at work. She's been married for thirty years."

Annie busted out laughing. I glanced at her, concerned for a second that she'd lost more than the cocktail of alcohol and cocaine that had been detoxed from her body. "What's so funny?"

"I'm just picturing some old bag with a construction hat clunking around in big tan steel-toed boots. Does she flirt with all the hot beefcakes that pound nails all day?"

I frowned at her. Sometimes Annie was extremely immature. "Maggie is very kind and great at her job. You would love her, I'm sure of it. So fucking judgmental."

"God. Still so touchy. Lighten up a little, Rio." She reached over and poked me in my ribs.

I moved away from her hand, the van moving just slightly as I took the steering wheel with me. "Me? I'm sorry. It's a bit hard to lighten up when I was called to come pick up my kid sister's best friend from her near-death experience."

"Well, at least I know now how you really feel."

"Yeah. A little angry with you. For doing this."

"This? What's this? Having fun?"

"Fucking up your life. You know what I mean."

"Yeah, I get it."

"Where am I taking you?"

"Just drop me off here! Jesus Christ!" She crossed her arms over her chest in defense, her lips puckered in a slight pout.

I sighed because it was obvious she had no place to go and I was it. We drove the rest of the way to my place in silence.

Stacy

After dropping Elly at her dorm and changing into appropriate clothes instead of Rio's hand-me-downs, I started the long arduous drive, once again, to my mother's. I didn't get very far before my gas light lit up. I pulled into the gas station and went through the motions of filling up my gas tank. My mind was reeling with Rio. I couldn't get him off the brain. All I could think of was his closeness, his smell, his smile. It had been nice, that relaxed playful moment we'd had together between when James had exploded and come back to apologize.

I smiled to myself as I got back into my car and turned it on. I was only a few miles down the road when the car started to sputter and then stopped completely. The momentum slowed as I pulled the car off to the side of the highway.

I glanced at the dashboard. There was nothing indicating that there was a problem of any kind but beyond what the car told me I had no idea what could possibly be wrong with it. "Shit." I quickly called my mother and waited for a long minute until it stopped ringing and her pre-recorded voice sounded in my ear.

"Mom. I'm not very far from Jonesboro and my car is broken down. I'm going to call someone for a ride but I just wanted to let you know that I might be late and not to worry. Love you."

I ended the call and then stared at my list of contacts as I scrolled through them. Elly was out, she didn't have a car. Kent was out, he was on his honeymoon. All the other names I saw were college friends who were all still out of town until classes started up again next week. When I reached the R's I sighed. Rio.

I put my phone in my lap and looked in my rearview mirror as if hoping someone would stop and help me. Maybe a knight in shining pickup truck or something. I exhaled deeply and pushed the "Call" button on my phone.

"Stacy. Everything ok?"

"Um...are you busy?" I bit my lower lip, secretly hoping that he was terribly busy and that he wouldn't be available to stop whatever he was doing to come rescue me.

"Not really, I just got out of the shower."

Oh God that was an image I didn't really need in my head right now. I shifted in my seat.

"What did you need, Stacy?"

Every time he said my name it sent shivers through me. His voice dripped of sex in its natural state but when he went breathy like that it just... I loudly cleared my throat and wished I had one of those coiled phone cords from my youth to wrap my finger around as I mustered up the courage to ask what I needed to ask.

"Um... I am kind of in a sticky situation and I was hoping you might be able to come get me?"

I heard shuffling and drawers closing on the other end of the line. "I will. Where are you?"

I looked around for anything to identify my exact location but there was nothing, not even a mile marker that I could see.

"Somewhere on I-38. I got off on an exit a few miles back to go to the gas station."

"Vague."

"I'm about twenty minutes out. Maybe thirty."

"Alright. Keep your phone on, I'll call you if I can't find you. And you call me if anything weird happens. And stay in your car so you don't get run over or kidnapped."

"Why would I be kidnapped? It's the middle of the day."

"You're an attractive woman all alone on a major highway vein, you could very easily be kidnapped."

I smiled at the acknowledgment from him that he thought I was attractive.

"Okay. I promise I will stay in the car with my doors locked."

"You might think about calling a tow truck too."

I was glad he mentioned that because I hadn't even thought past getting a ride.

"Well, maybe you could just stay where you are and the tow truck guy could give me a ride?"

"No!" He said it too quickly and with too much force. What did he have against tow truck drivers?

"O...kay."

"Call a local one so your car will be close."

"Okay, Mr. Bossypants."

He was silent for a long moment and I wondered if I'd said something to offend him.

"I'll be there soon, Stacy."

And with that he hung up the phone.

It was a little nerve wracking sitting in a car while cars kept whizzing past you at speeds of 65mph or more. Every van I saw I had hoped was Rio but it hadn't been yet. At least I hadn't thought so. I sighed as I put my head back against the headrest. I stared at the sun visor and noticed that there was a piece of paper sticking out from it.

I grabbed it and unfolded it, I didn't remember ever seeing it there before.

I love you. -C

I frowned at the note even as I wondered when he'd left it there for me. Had it been after we'd just had a fight? Had it been early on in our relationship?

I rolled down my window and started to rip up the note. I closed my eyes and put my hand out of the window, letting the note flutter onto the busy road. I opened my eyes to watch and screamed when my eyes met with Rio's disapproving stare. He grabbed my wrist and pushed my hand back into the car. His eyes moved to the traffic and once he thought it was safe he swung my door open and pulled me out of the car.

"What were you doing? You could've had your hand taken off."

He was being ridiculous. So much so that I couldn't help but laugh at him. This was possibly a mistake if his expression of irritation was any indication.

"I was getting rid of some baggage."

He looked like he wondered what my cryptic message had meant but he didn't ask for me to elaborate.

"Where is the tow truck guy?"

I shrugged my shoulders. "I don't know. I called him right after I spoke with you."

He glanced over my shoulders and then pushed me hard against my car, his body covering mine. My face was buried in the leather of his jacket and I inhaled the scent of him mixed with leather, my body on edge from the sudden movement. Rio pulled away, his face turned to the tow truck that had just arrived.

"Jesus, he almost ran us over," he growled before heading over towards the man disembarking from his vehicle.

My body was missing the warmth of his. I stayed by the hood of the car, watching and trying to clear my mind of the inappropriate thoughts and wishes. Like how I wished Rio could be the guy I could depend on and trust. And how I wished he weren't the bad boy player I was almost certain that he was.

I couldn't hear anything but from the body language being displayed I could only guess that Rio was yelling at my tow truck driver for nearly clipping him. I got into my car and pulled out my purse and phone before heading over towards them.

"You need to be more careful when you drive!"

"I was not even close to hitting you or your girlfriend, sir."

I cleared my throat before the argument could get blown way out of proportion. I held out my hand as I stepped around Rio.

"Hi. I'm Stacy. I'm the one who called for the tow. How does this work? Do I pay you now or later?"

"You'll pay me when you come to pick up your car, ma'am." His eyes flicked to Rio briefly. "Do you need a ride back into town?"

"No, that's what he is here for." I motioned over my shoulder to Rio who was shifting uneasily from one foot to the other.

The tow truck driver nodded his head and tilted his hat. "I'll just get your car all hooked up and then I'll be on my way. The office closes at 9pm, so if you need your car before that you'll need to make sure to come get it."

"You also have mechanics, don't you?"

"Yes, ma'am."

"I want them to take a look at it and call me when they figure out what's wrong with it and how much it's going to cost to fix it."

He nodded his head again and held out a clipboard. "Sure. I just need your information."

While I filled out the papers he got busy hooking up the car with Rio the guard dog watching his every move. Finally my car was on its way back home and I was left alone with Rio. We climbed into his van and started driving.

"Where to?" he asked, his eyes dutifully on the road.

"Oh, well, I was going to go to my mom's house but since the car broke down I figured I'd just go home."

"I can take you."

"No, really, that's okay, Rio."

His gaze turned and his eyes fell on me, freezing me to my seat. "I don't mind." He looked back to the road. "Just tell me where I'm going."

"Jonesboro."

He nodded. "Is that where you grew up?"

"Yep. Same trailer all my life." I wasn't exactly proud that we lived in a trailer park, but I was proud that my mom had provided a roof over my head. She did the best she could and that was all I could have asked for. She was the reason I'd gone to college. She was the reason I studied and worked really hard to get my degree. I wanted to be able to take care of her. I wanted to be able to break her dependence on men. I wasn't sure if it was entirely possible but I was going to try.

"What does your mom do?"

"She works at a diner."

He nodded a little. "My mom worked as a school secretary."

"And your dad?"

"My dad worked at the bar. He was a bartender."

"Was?"

"He hasn't had a job in years."

I watched as his jaw clenched and his knuckles turned white on the steering wheel. Obviously there was some bad blood between them but I didn't want to make this ride into anything unpleasant so I moved the conversation in a different direction.

"Who is your favorite band?"

He looked over at me, a look of surprise on his gorgeous features.

"That's a tough one. Would you laugh if I said The Backstreet Boys?"

I did laugh and placed one hand over it. "Yes, and I also wouldn't believe you. Not for a second."

"What? Their songs are so deep." He placed a large hand over his equally large chest.

"You are full of shit," I chuckled before pinching his outer thigh.

"Okay, okay." He grinned. "My favorite band would have to be Live."

I raised an eyebrow. "Live?"

He glanced at me a few times, "What's wrong with Live?"

"Nothing, I just pegged you more for–"

He didn't let me finish.

"For a death metal kind of guy."

I shrugged. Chance had loved Insane Clown Posse and Korn.

"What about you? Who is your favorite band?" he shot back, his question pulling me from yet another trip down memory lane with Chance's ghost.

"Um...probablyyyyy..." This was a hard question. I didn't want to give the wrong answer. I didn't want this musician to judge me based on my musical tastes but I had to let my freak flag fly free. "Me First and the Gimmie Gimmies."

"I've never heard of them."

I smiled, relieved. He couldn't pass judgement if he hadn't ever heard them before. "Elly and I have been to a few of their concerts. We always have a good time."

"Are they a big band?"

"Not Top 40 or anything. But they have a pretty decent following. They always play the smaller venues."

He nodded. "I'll have to check them out."

"Maybe you could go to one of their shows. They're coming to town in a few weeks."

He glanced at me again, grin on his lips. "Are you asking me out on a date?"

I looked over him and then huffed, "Maybe. I don't know if you'll even still be around in a few weeks."

"I'm not planning on skipping town. Unless I find out you're heinously evil."

"Really? That's it?"

"There are others, but I can't give away all my secrets."

Chapter 12

Rio

When we pulled up to the trailer I forced myself not to look at Stacy. She and I were more alike than she probably wanted to admit. I grew up in a place very much like this. In a shit ass neighborhood very much like this one.

"Thanks for the ride," she said, trying to avoid my gaze.

"I'll just wait out here for you. How long do you think you'll be?"

"What?" Her eyes widened in surprise.

Did she really think I was just going to leave her here?

"Stacy. You don't have a car. I'll give you a lift home. How long?"

She pushed the van door open and climbed out. "Just come on in. I can't leave you out here. The park will talk."

I smiled, inwardly freaking out about this huge step in our non-relationship. Meeting the parents. I slammed the door shut and made my way towards her. I rubbed my palms on my jeans, they were sweating like a motherfucker. I flashed a smile, hoping to reassure her that it was all going to be okay and to ease the tension I saw so easily in her shoulders.

She knocked on the door and after a minute a tall and rotund man answered the door. He was dressed only in boxers and wife beater. I wasn't sure when the last time the wife beater had been changed but it was sporting some yellow spots I would be very impressed by if they'd taken him less than 24 hours to grow.

"Stacy. What you doing here, girl?" The man looked over her with lusty eyes. I wrapped an arm around her shoulder and pulled her into my side.

"Hey. I'm Rio." I held my hand out and he shook it. I'd successfully averted his gaze from her. It was worth the greasy handshake.

"Hank, Stacy's step-daddy. Come on in, you two. Charlene is just getting herself a shower. She'll be right out. She was going to call you as soon as she was out, Stacy, to see if you still needed that ride. You should've called me, I woulda borrowed someone's truck to come get you."

"I didn't want to bother you," she said. Her body language was all wrong. She was tense and stiff. I got the firm impression that Hank was not a favorite of hers.

"Want a beer?" he offered to me.

"No, thanks. You want one?" I looked down at Stacy and she shook her head with a tiny smile as we stepped into the trailer, shutting the door behind us.

Hank headed into the kitchen and yelled down the hall as he opened the fridge. "WE GOT COMPANY!"

The man sure did have a set of pipes.

"So what do you do, son? You wasting money on a college education too?"

"Yes. But I wouldn't call it a waste."

"I got one. Never did nothin' for me." He grunted as he sat himself down in his recliner and popped the tab on his beer. He scratched his belly and motioned to the TV. "Y'all wanna watch the Steelers game too?"

"Um, no, thanks," Stacy said.

Hank glared at her. "You speak for him, girl?"

I felt her stiffen in my arms as his tone raised to one of warning.

"Yeah, she does," I said as I released her shoulders and moved my hand down to hers. I grasped it and gave it a little squeeze. She gave me a tight smile and pulled away as her mother came down the hallway. I could see where Stacy got her looks. Her mom was an older version of her with much shorter hair and a slightly thicker middle. She was hot.

"Baby girl!" Her mom wrapped her up in a warm hug before pulling away. Her eyes fell on me and took me in before glancing back at Stacy. "And who is this?" She sounded hopeful.

"Mom. This is Rio. He's my–"

I cut her off and stepped forward, offering my hand, "Her boyfriend." I caught Stacy's eye and nodded my head towards Hank, who was currently caught up in the football game. She gave me a frown before I continued. "So nice to finally meet you, ma'am."

Stacy's mom chuckled as she pumped my hand in greeting. "Don't ma'am me unless you've done somethin' wrong." She looked at Stacy. "You aren't pregnant, are you, honey?"

I felt the color leave my face as I watched Stacy's fill with color.

"What? Mom! No!"

Her mom, surprisingly, looked a little disappointed.

We chatted and helped with making dinner. Her mom was an easygoing woman. It was plain to see why Stacy loved her so much. When the subject of graduation popped up Stacy always diverted the conversation to something else. I made a mental note to ask her about it later.

We ate dinner in the same manner a normal family would until something happened. I wasn't sure what it was but I noticed the change in Stacy's demeanor right away.

I glanced between Stacy and Hank. He was staring right at her, looking like a cat with a canary in his mouth. What the fuck did I miss?

"Rio, next time you come remind me to tell you about the time Stacy had her boyfriend Chance over," he said, his words dripping with innuendo and seedy connotations.

I cleared my throat with a frown. Obviously this was not appropriate and he was just trying to make Stacy feel like shit.

"We have to go."

I set my silverware down and stood up from my chair. Stacy's eyes were wide as she stared up at me. Stacy's mom looked more regretful than anything. And Hank was furious that I wasn't taking his bait.

"Suddenly you have to get going? Seems kind of rude to get up and go in the middle of a meal, son."

"First of all, I'm not your son and second of all I'm not going to sit here while you try to humiliate Stacy. You're nothing but a fucking bully and I won't sit here and pretend I'm ignorant to it anymore. We're leaving."

Stacy stood up and went around to her mother and gave her a sideways hug. I nodded to her mom and ignored the belligerent blubbering from the bully as we walked to the door. We walked to the van and climbed in without words. I turned the key in the ignition and pulled out, heading for home.

Her silence was bothering me. Did I do the wrong thing? Had I overstepped my bounds?

The ride home was quiet, mostly because I didn't trust myself to open my mouth. What he'd done for me back there had been the most incredible thing any guy had every done for me. Chance would have never said anything against Hank he probably would have agreed and joined in poking fun at me so that he would fit in better with the other male in the room.

"What are you studying?" Rio asked, breaking into my thoughts.

"Accounting."

I saw the gears turning in his head as he mulled over what I'd just said.

"You graduate this spring, right? When do you start looking for jobs?"

"Well, I'm hoping I'll get an internship this summer. And if that goes well it could turn into a job offer. But if that doesn't pan out I'll intern somewhere near Jonesboro, probably, if not I'll just get a job straight out of college there."

"Jonesboro, huh?"

I glanced at him. "Yep. That's where my family is."

"I get it," he said softly before turning his attention back to the road.

Was he saying he understood why I wanted to be close to my mom who was married to that tool? Or did he understand that desire to be close to your family in general?

"What about you?"

"What about me?" he countered.

"What's your major?"

"Engineering."

"Engineering?!" Again, it had just slipped out. I slapped a hand over my mouth and then held my hands up in apology. "I'm so sorry."

He chuckled and shook his head, "It's okay, Stacy. Do you think you're the first person to react that way?"

I rubbed my neck which was suddenly feeling very warm. "Well, I shouldn't have been. No one should react that way. It's not fair to judge you or your intelligence or capability based on your appearance."

"I'm the engineer in disguise. They'll never see me coming." He chuckled again and I was glad he had a sense of humor about it but I wondered if that was how he actually felt or if this was a defense mechanism he put up to ward off anyone who might try to hurt him.

"Everyone will see you coming. It's hard not to see you coming."

"Oh Stacy. So dirty."

I wrinkled my brow in confusion and then gasped when his insinuation kicked in. "I didn't mean it like that, you pervert!" I chuckled and gave him a playful slap on his arm.

"Oh, baby. You know how I like it." He grinned at my embarrassment but it wasn't going to last long.

"I wish I did. God, I was so drunk that night. Maybe we should have a rematch."

His grin dropped and his jaw started to work under his skin.

I closed my eyes tightly to try to cover my horror at what I'd just said. Clearly he was just being playful with me like he probably did with all the other females in his life. "I was just kidding."

"I know," he said through gritted teeth. His face was bunched up with irritation, his knuckles held the steering wheel too tight. I wondered if he was angry because he'd thought we were moving into friendship territory and then I'd blown it by suggesting sex. But earlier he'd suggested sex. But maybe it was okay for him to suggest it but not me? I was so confused.

"Then why do you look so angry?"

"Because you were just kidding."

"But I thought you didn't want–"

He kept his eyes straight ahead as he cut me off. "I don't. You hungry?"

"What? We just had dinner at my mom's house."

"Oh, right."

Why did he look disappointed?

"But I could go for some dessert."

Chapter 13

Rio

I pulled off a few exits before ours to find a place to eat. I knew there probably weren't many places that she hadn't been but I wanted to make tonight end on a high note after what had happened. I pulled in alongside a row of shops. The downtown area of Chester wasn't much to talk about but the few businesses it did have had been here for a many years. Peggy's was one of those and there was a good reason why her shop was still here. She had the best pie, probably in the entire country.

We had to park a couple of blocks away because the parking lot was full, but it was nice to have a chance to walk alongside Stacy. I walked a little taller just knowing I was being seen with her. And not drunken Stacy, but sober Stacy. I had the urge to hold her hand but it was tucked at her side, holding onto the strap of her purse.

"You are going to be amazed."

"I won't," she said, giving me a little side grin.

"What? Why won't you be amazed?"

"I already know that Peggy's has the best pie."

The disappointment must have shown on my face because she started to laugh at me.

"Rio, come on. Everyone knows that. It's part of the speech they give at orientation. 'If you're ever feeling homesick you just need to catch a cab to Peggy's in Chester. It will make you feel like you're back in Grandma's kitchen.'"

"Well, shit. I was hoping to impress you."

She regarded me carefully. "You already have. I'm so sorry about Hank and the way he acted."

I felt the warming in my chest, the pride that she hadn't been angry about the Hank thing after all. We entered Peggy's and managed to snag the last table. We grabbed the menus and perused the daily pie selection until our waitress came over. After we ordered pie I sat back in my seat and put my hands on my thighs. Hers were on the table fiddling with a straw in its wrapper. I was tempted to touch her.

"An engineer. I still can't believe it."

I felt my lips curl into a smile. "Believe it. I'm not going to be poor Rio in a few years."

"Money isn't everything."

"It is when you don't have it."

She nodded, staring at her straw. "That's true enough. Most of the time money is what drives the wedge between my mom and her ...husbands."

"Mine never fought."

She looked up, surprised. "Really?"

I nodded. "Yep. Never. My dad didn't slip into the asshole persona until my mom died." Once her face started to soften and show signs of pity I looked away. I couldn't take that. Not from her. "After that he fought with me about money. He depended on me to make enough to support us. And when I moved out on my own he still tried to milk me for every cent I had."

She was quiet. When I glanced up that look of pity was still on her face.

"Did he pass away too?"

"No, he's still alive. I think."

"You think?"

I shrugged, "We had a falling out. I haven't spoken to him in a few years."

"That's so sad."

I clenched my teeth together. She had no idea what the hard part had been.

"So how long has your mom been married to Hank?"

"Ugh." I glanced up and tried not to show my relief that the pity was gone. "I don't know. Three years, I guess? I hope she's going to divorce him soon. Is that terrible of me to say?"

I shrugged my shoulder. "No. He's a dipshit. And I have a feeling there is something that happened between you two."

It was her turn to shrug and avoid my gaze. "He's just an asshole. He thinks it's okay to say anything he wants. My mom won't say anything. She needs a man to validate her. She has no self-worth." She glanced up and met my eyes. "And I don't want to ever be like that."

"And I don't want my whole life to revolve around one woman either. I don't want to end up like my dad. He was crushed and beaten down and depressed when she left him."

She shook her head, "I don't think that's possible."

I took my time taking everything about her in from her wind-blown curls to her expressive eyes, her pink cheeks, to her slightly pouty lips. She had no idea how wrong she was.

Stacy

I swallowed back my anxiousness as we sat in his van, still vibrating with life beneath us, and stared at each other in the darkness. "Thanks for today. It was much easier to handle with you by my side." I felt like such a cheese head for saying it but it made him grin a little so it had been worth it.

"Thanks for calling me." He reached out and put his hand against my jaw and rubbed my cheek with the pad of his thumb. His thumb worked over my cheek again, but this time slower as his eyes stared at my lips. His lips parted and slowly closed the distance between us. I was frozen in place, eagerly awaiting the feel of his mouth against mine again. In my mind I kept thinking that this wasn't actually going to happen, that it had to be some sort of trick but as the seconds passed by his mouth grew closer and closer until it finally captured mine.

We both groaned with pleasure as we stretched across the distance between our seats. My hand went to his hair, grabbing onto it to hold him to me. I didn't want this moment between us to end. I didn't want anything to come between us. I didn't want him to stop kissing me. And he didn't. He groaned again, his other hand reaching into my hair, grabbing a bunch to hold me to him.

Our mouths danced together and wetness gathered underneath my jeans. He broke the kiss only to whisper.

"Fuck. Stacy, we shouldn't be doing this."

"But I want to," I whispered back.

"It isn't going to end well. I'm not ready but I just..." He groaned, his lips had spent too much time away from mine so I reclaimed them, kissing him passionately, forcing my tongue between his teeth to dance over his.

He grabbed onto my hair and pulled my head back, exposing my neck which he licked from the crevice to my ear. I shivered in my seat, my nipples were aching, begging to be free and in his mouth. I gasped when his hot mouth closed around my earlobe and then released it, the cold air replacing his warmth.

"Rio..." I wasn't sure if I was going to ask him for something or beg.

He growled as his kisses moved down my neck again, his hand pulled my sweater down so he could kiss my chest. The sweater didn't allow him the access that he wanted so he growled and settled for squeezing me over my sweater. I groaned, my panties getting wetter by the second. I shifted uncomfortably, he made a ache between my legs.

With me leaning towards him he popped the buckle on my seatbelt, releasing me to come closer. Like a moth to a flame I closed the distance, straddling him in his seat so that our hot centers were pressed together. After I mounted him I grabbed onto his hair and held on tight as I kissed him and rubbed myself shamelessly against his hard length which was still hiding under the denim of his jeans.

His large hands wrapped around my back, under my sweater, his body heat warming me ten times more than the sweater itself ever could. I moaned in ecstasy as the friction between us started to arouse me higher. Like the raising of the tempo in a classical piece by Strauss my excitement raised to a crescendo which abruptly fell when Rio's phone rang in his pocket, cutting the string of tension that had been building between us. With ragged breaths we reluctantly unglued ourselves from one another.

I pushed my hair out of my face as he pulled the phone from his pocket. The name flashed at me in the darkness before I could look away. Annie. I felt my cheeks heat and looked away.

"I should take this," he said. He was about to get out of the van when I opened my door. I didn't want him to have to get out and take a call from another girl and then get back in. The awkwardness would only be increased.

"Sure. I'll see you later," I said with more certainty than I was feeling. Who was Annie? He looked torn as I shut the door behind me but it was better this way. I waved and then turned away before I did something I would later regret. I didn't look back. I couldn't.

What if he was Chance and I was the other woman? What if Annie was the girl he was seeing and he was trying to capture me, love me, use me and then toss me away when Annie found out and threatened to leave him?

When I got into my tiny studio apartment I changed into my PJs and hopped into bed. Tears spilled down my cheeks at the realization that I'd built Rio up in my mind and let him get close. And he wasn't unlike what I'd thought he was. He was just like Chance. I had to choose to guard myself better the next time he tried to use me.

Chapter 14

Rio

I stared at Stacy's retreating form. Fuck it all! I didn't know what had come over me and I had mixed feelings about what had just happened. It had been earth tilting but so wrong. I wasn't supposed to be getting mixed up with her. Not yet. I couldn't keep the growl out of my voice when I answered my phone. "Annie. What is it?"

"You have no food in your fridge and you said you were going to get groceries like six hours ago. I just wanted to make sure you weren't dead."

"That's touching."

"Look, man, my stomach is rumbling and the bar down the road is calling my name. So if you don't want me to go on another bender you better come home with hot food in your mitts. You have thirty minutes."

"Forty. I'm on my way." I hung up the phone and stared regretfully at Stacy's building. I saw her light turn on, saw her move about her apartment. When she disappeared again I pulled away, heading for the Thai carry-out restaurant.

I arrived back at my house in thirty-eight minutes. As soon as I walked in Annie assaulted me, grabbing the bag of food from my hand.

"Thank God!"

She took off running towards the kitchen table and unpacked the paper bag quicker than a kid opening their present from Santa at Christmas.

She snagged the container of pad thai, went to get a fork and then she took it into the living room and plopped herself down on the floor to eat it. I walked over and glanced at the TV. Some stupid chick flick. I'd never understand the appeal.

"Hurry, Rio! It just started!"

I rolled my eyes and took my time gathering my food before joining her in the living room.

"What the fuck is this?"

"When Harry Met Sally. It's a classic."

I sighed and debated going into the kitchen to eat in peace but then Meg Ryan started making orgasm sounds, drawing my attention towards the screen. She was good at that. I plopped myself down on the couch and got lost for a couple of hours.

By the end of the movie I was staring at Annie as she wiped away tears. "So good," she muttered, shaking her head. "Way to go, Harry."

I couldn't believe I'd just lost two hours of my life to that movie. Ah well. I cleared my throat as I stood up and reached down for her trash. She handed it to me and studied my face.

"You didn't cry? Not at all?"

I frowned at her. What a crazy woman. "No. Not at all. He was a dumbass for not realizing sooner that he had a thing for her."

And then she was frowning right back at me. "I forgot I was talking to Mr. I'm-Never-Going-To-Get-Married-Because-I-Have-Daddy-Issues."

"Fuck you, too," I grumbled as I cleaned up after us. My phone rang again and I fished it out of my pocket. It was Elly. "What's up?"

"I just got off the phone with Stacy. That was so nice of you to give her a ride! You like her."

It wasn't a question so I didn't think I had to answer. "Is that all you wanted to say?"

"No. Since her car is broken I'm going to need a ride to practice."

"Yeah, sure, no problem. Just text me your address so I can look at directions."

"Thanks, Rio. What a pal you are."

"Yeah. That's me, buddy. I'll see you tomorrow, Els."

"K. Night, Rio!"

After I hung up I turned around and sharply exhaled when my eyes landed on Annie who had been standing right behind me, eavesdropping. "Jesus Christ."

"Who was that?" Her finger was around the ends of her hair, twirling it slowly around her finger.

I frowned and hoped my sour expression would make her back off. "What?"

"Who was on the phone? It sounded like a girl." She took a step closer and I shook my head and moved around her, throwing away the trash. I heard her feet on the linoleum as she followed behind me.

"That's because it was a girl."

"Oooh. I knew there was some dirt you were keeping from me. How long have you two been fucking?"

Her crass language didn't exactly affect me. I'd been hearing cuss words from her since she was nine. My mother used to try and change Annie's mouth, the only thing she'd really managed to do was curb Annie's language when she was in the vicinity. It was good enough for my mom. "Annie. We aren't fucking but even if we were, it's none of your goddamn business. Jesus."

"Is she hideous?"

I sighed. She was going to pester me all night if I didn't give her some reason not to. "No. She isn't hideous, but I'm not interested in her. She's the new singer in the band."

"Damn. So... does that mean you're absolutely single?"

I got a weird feeling in the pit of my stomach. My palms started to sweat. "Yes?"

She stepped around to the front of me and I tried to step back but my ass met with the counter. She'd cornered me. Her palms went to my chest. I was so shocked I just stood there like a dumbass.

"Good." She stared at me, a little smile on her lips as her hands moved down the front of my body. I grabbed them just as they reached the belt line.

"Woah. Annie. You're like a little sister to me."

The disappointment was thick on her face. "Damnit. I'm just so horny."

"Join the club. But it's not going to happen, Annie. Not with us. Never."

"What about that guy? The dude that plays drums?"

"James?" I was confused and relieved as she stepped back, putting space between us once again. She really was just horny, she didn't have those feelings for me. It was a load off my mind. I tried to picture James and Annie together. The thought made my stomach churn.

"Yeah. Do you think he would be interested?"

I put my hands over my ears. "Disgusting. I'm going to take a shower and then I'm going to bed."

"Okay, but if you change your mind you know where to find me."

She slapped my ass as I passed her. I wondered just how long she was going to be crashing with me because I knew I wouldn't have the heart to kick her out before she was ready. I owed it to Penny.

Stacy

It had been weeks since I'd last seen Rio. Truth be told I was avoiding him. The mechanic had long since diagnosed my car problems (it turns out that putting diesel in your non-diesel tank is not a good idea) but I didn't currently have the money to get it fixed so I was off the hook for driving Elly to and from her band practice, which she engaged in at least three times a week. She never mentioned Rio when we talked and I never asked. I didn't want her to know how far I'd fallen with him and I didn't want to know if he'd moved on since then. I certainly hadn't. He was all I could think about and every corner I turned I swore I saw him, but it was never him.

I finished up my makeup and pressed my lips together to make sure the lipstick was even before I moved away from the bathroom mirror and gathered my purse. Even tonight I was thinking of him as I readied myself for the concert I had casually mentioned to him. My phone remained silent so I figured whatever had been going on with him and Annie was on again, not off again.

Elly called me and I headed downstairs. I smiled at the taxi parked on the curb and took a peek to confirm it was her before I got in. I saw her face but the other hiding in the darkness was a complete surprise.

"Kent?"

He flashed me an innocent smile from the middle seat. "Hey Stacy. Hope you don't mind my crashing the girls' night."

"Um, no, I guess not. We aren't getting makeovers, we're going to a concert."

I wanted to give Elly a look and a slap on arm for allowing this to happen but she was safely on the other side of Kent and not looking at me. I got in, shut the door and placed my purse in my lap. The taxi lurched forward without much warning throwing me against the door. I grabbed onto the side handlebar and ignored the pain until it subsided when Kent got his bearings and moved back to his seat.

"I'm so excited!" Elly said, her shoulders bobbing up and down.

"Me too," Kent said. I watched in silence as Kent's hand moved to Elly's knee. She smiled at Kent and plucked his hand from her knee and put it back into his own lap.

It was my turn to smile. Good for her. Somewhat sticking to her boundaries.

"How is married life?" I asked Kent.

Kent grinned, "Oh, it's pretty much the same. Except for this." He pointed to the golden ring on his finger.

"You'll probably attract more women with that thing on, you know."

He blushed and politely shook his head. "Nah. The girls don't pay me any attention."

Elly scoffed as she gazed out her window at the scenery passing us by. "More like you don't pay them any attention."

"What can I say?" he said, "I have all the ladies I need already. Why would I look for more?" He pointed at us with his thumbs and we both shook our heads.

When we arrived at the 11:30 Club there was already a line assembling outside. Kent paid for the cab and then we piled out of the taxi and joined at the end of the line.

"Wow. I had no idea there would be so many people," he said.

"Me First and the Gimmie Gimmies are good, Kent, I told you!" Elly said as she came to a stop behind a couple who had their hands in each other's back pockets.

I watched with disappointment as they both took in the couple, then each other, then looked away as if they hadn't just been thinking the exact same thing about each other.

"I'm gonna go scope the crowd and see if anyone else ahead of us might let us stand with them. I want to be near the stage." I left Elly and Kent alone to be with their ridiculous selves. They weren't going to ruin my night. I walked alongside the line slowly, taking in faces, hoping someone would be familiar enough to at least chat with for a few minutes while we waited out the line.

I had reached the end when the tall long haired guy in a leather jacket with his back to me gave me pause. It couldn't be. The bouncer and Rio both laughed. My breath caught in my throat as his eyes met mine.

"Stacy! Hey," he waved me to come closer so I did and let his arms wrap around me in a hug as he kept one foot in the line to keep his place.

"Hey," I said as I pulled away and looked between the bouncer and Rio. "What are you doing here?"

"Some chick invited me a few weeks ago but she never called me to confirm. I think she stood me up."

I laughed softly, my cheeks flaming with guilt and shame. "She probably figured since you were a man that you'd call her. Especially after you dropped her off at her front door without so much as a promise of something more."

It was his turn to look ashamed. "Yeah. About that." He rubbed the back of his neck nervously.

I held up my hand to stop him from talking before he got too far. I didn't want to hear about him and Annie. Or whatever he was going to tell me. I didn't want him to ruin my night. As long as she wasn't here I could pretend Rio and I were the only two people in the room. I wasn't going to let him make the moves on me again but just being next to him was enough for me. He made me feel safe and happy. "Nope. There's no need to explain." I smiled but he didn't take the hint.

"I do need to explain, I–" Before he could finish the bouncer unhooked the rope and held his hand out for Rio's ticket. He grabbed my hand and pulled me into line beside him and handed the bouncer his ticket. Mine was already out so he took mine too. After ripping them in half he pushed us through the door. It was dark inside, dimly lit enough to see if someone was standing in front of you but most of the light was directed onto the bar which is where my gaze was when Rio's voice sounded in my ear soft and tantalizing.

"Do you want something to drink?"

I looked over my shoulder and shook my head. "No, I'm good. Do you?"

He shook his head too. "Come on, let's go upstairs so we can talk for a minute before things get too rowdy."

I'd never been the first in line before and I kind of wanted to stand at the stage. I glanced at the stage longingly and I heard a soft chuckle from my companion.

When I glanced at him he was smiling down at me. "You really want to go up there in the mosh area? You'll get squished."

"Please? It's not really that kind of crowd." I begged, batting my eyelashes for all that they were worth.

"Alright," he replied, amusement still in his tone. "But when some other guy is pressing you against the stage don't expect me to jump in and save you."

I felt my mouth drop into a pout. He winked at me. "Because some girl will probably have me pressed against the stage too."

I chuckled and walked to the front of the club. I stood with my back to the stage and looked around him to the people flooding into the door. "I hope Elly isn't waiting for me out there." I pulled out my phone and dialed her number. It rang a few times before going to voicemail. I wondered if she had it on silent or if she was ignoring my calls. I sighed and stared at the door again.

"So, about the goodnight kiss the other night..." Rio started.

Chapter 15

Rio

Her grin and frantically waving arm stopped the words I needed to say from coming out. I turned and saw Elly walking in, looking as sparkling as usual, and some dude on her heels. He looked vaguely familiar and it took me a minute to place him. That was the dude from the bar and the wedding. I frowned. What the hell was he doing here? That must have been the shortest marriage in history. Okay, maybe not all of history, but it had been pretty damn short. Like a month?

I waited until they approached to move next to Stacy. Resisting her had already been harder than I'd thought it was going to be. I had missed her smile. I'd wanted to call her but I hadn't managed to find the right words to explain the situation and then the semester started. I was an asshole for having so many excuses but the truth of it was that I was scared to open that door to her. I was scared to let her pull me into her world. I was scared to let her get close to me. I was scared that once she knew the truth about my family, about me, about my sister, that she would realize just how much baggage I carried around with me.

"Rio! What are you doing here?" Elly's arms wrapped me up in a friendly hug, which I returned and then set her back on her feet.

"Stacy invited me."

Elly gave Stacy a look that meant Stacy hadn't been kissing and telling. I don't know why but that warmed me. "She did, did she?"

Stacy rolled her eyes. "I mentioned the concert, that was all. And I was right at the front when the line started to move and I ran into Rio. I tried calling you but

I got your voicemail."

"Hmm, must not have heard it." She shrugged her shoulders and then looked behind her to the bar. "Does anyone else want a beer? I'm going in!"

Stacy and I smiled politely but refused.

"I'll go with you," Kent said, a warm smile on his lips.

I shook my head and looked away. The man was a fucking idiot. Anyone could see that the love in his eyes aimed towards Elly was not in a sisterly way. I looked down at Stacy after they'd moved away and she started to laugh at me.

"What?" I crossed my arms over my chest.

She shook her head. "Nothing. I just think that we see the same thing when it comes to those two."

I glanced at Elly and Kent who were leaning close and talking into each other's ears.

"I think everyone sees the same thing when it comes to those two. Except for him. Was he dropped on his head as a baby?"

Stacy snorted and promptly covered her mouth and nose with her hands, her wide green doe eyes staring up at me.

Holy hell. I wanted to hear that again.

"Did you just snort?"

She shook her head, her cheeks flushed a tempting shade of pink. "No, you must be hearing things, old man."

I couldn't help but grin at her mild teasing. "Maybe so. It's hard to hear much past the constant tinnitus."

"Oooh, such a big word."

"I'm older and wiser, young lady. I know lots of big words."

"Oh? Like what?"

I leaned down and put my lips just out of reach of her ear and whispered. "Osculator, which is what you are. One who kisses." I smiled to myself as she wiggled beside me.

Her chest was moving more rapidly underneath her sweater. "And you are extremely callipygian."

I pulled back and stared at her, wondering what the word meant. "What the hell does that word mean?"

She just smiled and turned her fingers against her lips and tossed the imaginary key over her shoulder. I shook my head, a grin on my lips. I loved how playful she could be and how at ease she made me.

"You do not play fair, Miss."

"Neither do you, Mister."

We talked more while we waited for the show to start but there never seemed to be just the right time to explain Annie. How does one explain Annie? How does one explain what she represents for me? I wasn't sure I was ready for Stacy to see me as I saw myself. As a failure and a horrible big brother. I never wanted her opinion of me to be bad. I was afraid that once she knew the real me she'd run - fast and far. And I wouldn't blame her.

Elly and Kent came back, interrupting further conversation.

"So I hear you guys have another wedding gig coming up?" Kent asked, stepping closer to close in our little circle. It was getting loud and crowded as the patrons waiting for the show to start up.

I nodded, my eyes dancing between the three of them. "Yeah. And another one a couple of weeks after that."

Elly smiled as her beer dropped from her lips. "I'm excited to see my guys in tuxes again. They rocked them, didn't they, Stacy?"

Stacy's eyes darted away from me as soon as I caught her staring at me. "Yeah, they definitely did. Whose wedding? Do I know them?"

Elly shook her head. "No. Friends of Jen's father."

Kent shifted a bit at the mention of his wife's name. He reached over and grabbed onto Elly's beer. "I changed my mind. Give me a little of that." She loosened her hold and he brought the bottle to his lips. I glanced away, my eyes studying Stacy. She watched the two with slight venom in her gaze. I understood it. What was Kent doing here with Elly anyway? Why would Elly still be hanging out with him? She must have been a fan of pain. Of course who was I to judge her? I was here with Stacy and it was just as painful to be here with her and keep my hands to myself.

The lights darkened further on the main floor as a group of men came to the center of the stage. We all joined in the crowd, clapping to welcome the musicians. I had no idea what I was in for but anything would be better than watching the unrequited feelings that were all around.

During the show I saw a side of Stacy that I hadn't had a glimpse of since the night we first met at the bar. She was bouncing and playful and free. She had let her guard down and let herself go. I drank it up the way I used to down six packs of beer in my bedroom while my dad was rambling and yelling at the empty couch about my mother and how much he wished he'd never laid eyes on her.

When the show was over we were all exhilarated and high from Stacy's favorite band which, I had to admit, put on a pretty damn good show. It was like going to a karaoke bar but everything was played with a metal twist. And the guys, just plain dudes, were getting paid to do what they loved. I admired that about them and I knew that I'd be buying at least one of their CDs before the week was over.

I put my hands on Stacy's shoulders as she led the way through the crowd that was hastily exiting. We piled out of the door and started walking down the street, letting the cool air work its magic on our overheated bodies, Stacy came to an abrupt stop. The man standing in front of her was only slightly shorter than I was, his dark hair was slicked back with gel, his eyes outlined with a light layer of eyeliner. He looked at Stacy as if he had possession of her. His dark eyes roamed over her body slowly, like he was very familiar with her.

I didn't like it. Not one bit.

My heart was just about beating out of my chest as I stared into the eyes of the man who had caused me so much torture since I'd started college and got wrapped up in him.

"Chance."

His eyes roamed over my body and I realized as he did it that I didn't feel the flutters and excitement that I used to feel. Instead I felt... anger. "Stacy. You're looking good. How are you doing?"

His gaze didn't break away from mine, not even when I looked away, feeling Rio shifting behind me.

"I'm doing fine, thanks. How about yourself?"

He shrugged his broad shoulders, "I'm okay. The band and I are making waves, heading out west on a little mini-tour."

I smiled politely, "That's great, Chance."

Rio shifted again, I felt his hand move to my lower back as he cleared his throat loudly. I looked over my shoulder at him. His eyes gave me a dark look that told me that he didn't like this guy. I wondered if it was because he could tell he was my ex or because he knew that Chance had bad written all over him.

"Um, Chance, this is Rio. Rio, my ex, Chance."

Chance nodded his head, flicking his gaze to Rio for the tiniest of acknowledgement and then turned his gaze back to me, talking as if Rio weren't even there. "So this is your new boy toy, Stacy? The Chance replacement? It looks like you downgraded."

I felt Rio attempt to lurch forward but I grabbed his arm and squeezed. Chance's eyes looked amused at how easy it was to ruffle Rio's feathers.

"I didn't need a Chance replacement."

"True," he said nodding, his eyes still taking in my body, "you can have me whenever you want me. You know that, don't you, Stacy?"

Rio tried to pull away but I still held him tightly to my side. "I do. But I don't want you. Never again." I lifted my nose in the air and stepped around him, Rio at my side, his neck turned around, staring daggers at the man whom I had once thought I loved.

"I don't like that guy," he said, when we were far enough away that Chance wouldn't overhear.

"I don't like him much either."

"Anymore. But you did, didn't you?"

I looked up at him, his judgement making me feel like I was less of a person for falling for someone like Chance. I withdrew my hand from him and crossed my arms over my chest, suddenly feeling very cold.

"Stacy," he groaned as he tried to wrap his arm around my shoulders.

I sidestepped him and shook my head. "I did. I did like him. I thought I loved him. But that was then. I've learned from my mistakes." My eyes met his, they were full of regret. Probably the regret of being here with me, of thinking that I was some princess with expensive taste. The truth was that I liked the trash, just like my mother, bless her heart. I couldn't help myself it seemed. I was attracted to the bad boys. "It was good to see you at the concert. Drive safe." I offered him a tight smile. He fell out of step beside me. When I looked back his moody eyes were on me. He ran his hands through his hair in frustration.

"Stacy!" He jogged to catch up but didn't try to touch me again. "I'm not going to let you walk around town in the middle of the night by yourself. My bike is right around the corner. Let me take you home."

I hesitated, "I don't know where Elly is."

"She was walking the other way with Kent when you were giving your ex fuck-me eyes."

My temper was starting to rise. "Excuse me? I was not giving him fuck-me eyes."

"You were. But that's fine. I get it."

I regarded him carefully. "Are you jealous?" He stared at me with disinterest but I knew it was a facade. He was jealous. Inside I felt giddy at the thought. Outwardly I hid it. I sighed softly and then shrugged. "Okay. Fine. Let me just text Elly and let her know I'm going to get a ride from you."

After I was done texting, he strapped his helmet onto my head and climbed onto his motorcycle. I stared at him while he grinned at me. "Hop on."

I shook my head. "I'm going to fall off."

"Mr. Rockstar didn't have a motorcycle?" He gaped in disbelief for a second before shaking his head. "Look, just climb on behind me and put your arms around my middle." He pointed to a little rod coming out from the side of the bike, "That's for your feet. Don't move your legs backwards or miss that thing or you're going to burn yourself."

"Sounds real safe," I muttered as I climbed onto the back of his bike. I held on tightly, pressing my cheek between his shoulder blades. His body vibrated and bounced as he chuckled, presumably at me, but I didn't care. I didn't feel like dying tonight.

His body lurched and then the bike came to life beneath us, vibrating and purring. I closed my eyes tightly and continued to hold him with a death grip. One of his hands covered mine and then gave it a gentle pat before we started to move. To my relief he wasn't showing off for me. He wasn't weaving in and out of traffic, he wasn't making the bike shift left or right to any extremes. Just before we reached my apartment I lifted my head and chanced a look behind us. We were all alone on the street. For some reason that gave me a huge chill.

He came to a stop on the curb and switched off the bike. After a few seconds I released him and climbed off the bike. My knees felt like Jell-o. That was maybe one of the scariest things I'd ever done. I didn't do much outside of my comfort zone.

I tried to take the helmet off but I couldn't manage to figure out the straps. He chuckled at me and wiggled his finger for me to come to him after he'd swung his leg around. His ass was leaning against his bike seat, his legs splayed open for me to move between them. I swallowed hard as I moved between his warm, strong legs and held my chin up so that he could undo the straps.

He removed the helmet and then held it tucked under his arm. His handsome face smiled down at me and I felt my knees grow weaker.

"Safe and sound."

"Thanks, Rio."

"Anytime, Stacy. I had fun tonight." I went to take a step back but his hand reached out and took my hand, holding it gently in his. "I've missed you."

I pressed my lips together, almost not believing what I was hearing. "I've missed you too." I hadn't wanted to admit it, but I couldn't lie to him.

There was nothing else said. It was as if those words were the magic password that let the gravity between us pull us closer. My body melded to his and our lips did their familiar heated dance, dialing up the passion, leaving us both breathless.

When my knees started to wobble I pulled back and whispered, "Do you want to come in?"

He glanced over my shoulder at the apartment and then back to my face. His eyes took me in as his response battled in his head. "I do. But I shouldn't." He pressed a kiss to my forehead and then let me go. Without him holding me I wasn't sure I could stand but after his rejection I had to make sure I was doing all I could to stand on my own two feet.

I nodded and dropped my gaze. "Night." I turned on my heel and started walking to the door, my keys in my hand shaking softly. I fumbled with the lock for a minute before I felt heat at my back. My hand stilled and Rio's large hand took the keys from me. With ease and assurance I was far from feeling he stuck the key in the door. The lock clicked open with the turn of the key. I could feel the presence of his body behind mine. I longed to feel his hard muscles pressed against me. I closed my eyes, I could hear my soft pants echo back to me from the door.

"Can I have a do-over?" he asked, his voice husky and low.

My mind was fogging over the longer he stood behind me. "Do you want to come in?" I licked my lips, which suddenly felt very dry.

His hand turned the doorknob and pushed the door open. I barely registered that it had banged against the fridge because Rio's arms had come around me, pressing me against his body while his lips started to assault my neck. I closed my eyes, soaking up the enigma that was him. I held onto his elbows as he walked us into my apartment. His lips moved away from my neck and I heard myself protest.

"Do you want something to drink? Water?" he asked, straightening himself up, his hands now buried into his pockets.

I opened my eyes and looked around my apartment. It was a mess and the realization that this was what he was seeing caused me to pull away. "I wasn't expecting company," I picked up three pieces of clothes from the floor before he pulled me back up and came around to look at me. There was a grin on his lips. "What's so funny?"

"Nothing," he said as he grabbed the clothes from my hands and dropped them back onto my floor. I was about to protest when he lifted my chin, forcing me to look at him. "I love seeing how you really live. I don't want the polished up version of you. I want the real you."

I felt a blush color my cheeks. I wanted desperately to look away but I forced myself to keep his gaze. I was rewarded with another kiss, his arm tightening around my waist, pulling me in closer to his body.

The wetness pooled between my legs, ripping a moan from me as I held onto him. I wasn't sure what was going to happen next but I knew what I wanted to happen and judging by the hardness in his pants I had a feeling he wanted the same thing too. He backed me up until my lower back was against the one kitchen counter I had. He lifted me up. His intention was to put me up there. I knew it was messy so I winced at the thought.

"No, no. Bed."

At least there weren't crumbs there, I hoped.

He growled and held onto me, his hands cupped under my ass. I wrapped my legs around him and devoured his lips once again. He matched me kiss for kiss and then lowered me onto my bed. I pushed a big pile of clothes onto the floor. He ground himself against me, teasing me. I purred. I was beyond ready for this.

Chapter 16

Rio

"I haven't been able to get you out of my mind," I said as I stared down at her. I lowered myself to her neck, pressing a kiss there, making her shiver beneath me. I moved my kisses down the center of her body, heading for the place that filled my dreams at night. I was at the waist of her jeans when my phone started to ring in my back pocket.

I huffed out a hard breath, undecided whether I should ignore it or pick it up. What if it were an emergency? Annie. Fuck. I moved back up and kissed Stacy hard. I didn't want her running away. I wanted her to want me. And I was sure she wanted me in that moment.

I pulled my phone from my pocket and glanced at the screen. It was Annie. I glanced at Stacy with regretful eyes. "I'm sorry, Princess. I've gotta take this." She stared back at me with a mixture of what I knew was confusion and disbelief. I was gladly going to have to make that up to her.

I answered the phone and walked over to Stacy's single window and glanced out at my bike, still parked and all alone on the street. "Hello?"

"Rio, are you busy?"

I could tell by the wobble in her voice that she was drunk. Drunk I could deal with, but if she were high on top of it, which she probably was, she was a danger to herself.

"Where are you?"

"Tippy's or Pippy's or something like that I think." She giggled. "Sippy's?"

I tried to release the annoyance I was feeling. I was so close to bridging the gap with Stacy. I glanced over my shoulder, Stacy had gotten up from the bed and was walking around her studio apartment plucking her clothes from the floor. She was moving so slowly and quietly, I was sure she was eavesdropping.

"Okay. Stay put. I'm coming to get you."

"LOVE YOU!"

I pulled the phone away from my ear to save my hearing but by the look on Stacy's face I knew that she'd heard it too. I ended the call and shoved my phone back into my pocket.

"That was just a friend. She's a little on the wild side."

She shrugged her shoulders as if she didn't care but I could tell that she did. It had been one month of sobriety and after speaking with Tom about things he said I could ease myself into a relationship. It had been one month since I'd had Stacy's mouth beneath mine, one month since I'd touched her and made her crazy with the flick of my tongue. In that moment I really wished that Annie was at my house safe and sound so that I could finish what I'd started here. But she wasn't and I couldn't stay for fear that Annie would do something stupid, like OD... again.

"I hate to leave but I have to go take care of this."

"Sure. Go leave and pick up the girl who screams that she loves you. Totally cool with me."

I closed the distance between us and held her face in my hands, forcing her to look me in the eyes. I saw pain there and it ripped at my heart. I didn't want her to hurt. Not because of me.

"She is just a friend. She doesn't do to me the things that you do, Stacy. And if I didn't feel like I had to do this I wouldn't be leaving. But I do."

There was a look of confusion on her face again.

"Why?"

I stared at her, she was searching my face for answers. Searching for secrets that I wasn't ready to disclose. Not yet.

"Because I do. I owe it to someone." I kissed her, hard, branding her lips with mine so that she would have a hard time going to bed tonight without thinking about me and all the things my kiss promised her. "I'll call you later."

She bit her lower lip and nodded as I let her go.

"Thanks for the ride."

I grinned, tucking some of her hair behind her ear. "Anytime. Good night, Stacy."

Without another word I left her apartment before I decided against leaving. Lord knew I could stay in Stacy's bed for days. It would take that long to get the edge off.

Stacy

I tucked my hand behind my neck as I stared at the open textbook in front of me. My last semester of college. I couldn't believe it. Only one more semester of books and lectures and papers. One more semester of Elly. And Rio.

Three days had passed and I still hadn't heard anything from him. My mind was busy wondering if he was okay or if he had changed his mind about kissing me. I had been surprised by his sudden desire to touch me. Was he getting lonely again? Had he had a fight with that Annie girl or had he just been using me? One thing was certain, I was not going to let him kiss me again until he told me the whole story. I could tell he'd been holding something back. Why was he hesitating in telling me? What was he hiding?

My eyes drifted away from the textbook and stared at my cellphone. Studying wasn't going to happen if I didn't get Rio off of my mind. I exhaled loudly and then grabbed my phone. I dialed his number before I lost my nerve and then pressed the phone to my ear. I turned down my study music when a voice came on the line.

"Hello?"

The voice was not his. Definitely not his unless he'd recently been kicked very hard in the balls. Even then I don't think his voice could reach the same pitch of the woman who had answered his phone.

"Hi. I'm trying to reach Rio."

"He's busy. Call back tomorrow." I heard his laugh in the background just before the phone disconnected.

I tried to ignore the feeling of heavy disappointment in my chest. I put my phone down and forced myself to concentrate on the book in front of me. I had tried to reach out to him. I wasn't used to being the one chasing the boys. The boys used to chase me. There was only one guy before Rio who I'd chased - Chance. And he'd broken my heart. All the old feelings came flooding back along with the memories of Chance and whoever he'd cheated on me with. I wondered briefly if Annie was blonde like the girl who'd been sucking Chance's dick. I felt my eyes water and quickly brushed away the hot tears.

I deserved better than a guy who felt he could just run into me and get me into his bed. And I deserved to be chased. I shut my textbook and went to my closet. I wasn't going to stay home and mope over the loss of him. I'd never even really had him. It was happy hour and I wanted to feel happy. After changing into something that I knew would garner male attention, I grabbed my purse and headed for the bar.

On the way I'd dialed Elly but she couldn't make it. I was forced to face the fact that I really only had one friend here at college. I played nice with other girls that I'd had classes with but I didn't ever really hang out with them or make an effort to get closer to them. So here I was, going out to the bar, alone. I shrugged it off. I was going to the bar alone but I wouldn't be leaving alone. Not if my boobs had anything to say about it. Once I fucked Rio out of my system I would finally be able to concentrate on getting my studying done. I only had one semester left. I wasn't going to blow it for some guy who couldn't seem to pick up the phone and call.

Chapter 17

Rio

I was sitting on my couch with Annie when my stomach started to growl. I didn't feel like cooking and it was getting late. "I'm gonna order a pizza. Pepperoni okay?"

She tore her eyes away from the couch as I stood up and nodded. "Sure." I was walking away when she called out. "Oh! Some girl called you earlier. I told her to call back later because we were busy watching TV."

I paused and then shook my head. It was probably just Elly. I grabbed up my phone and checked the call log. Damn. It had been Stacy. I felt a tinge of regret deep in my belly. I had wanted to call her for the past few days but every time I picked up the phone Annie called me to do something for her. She had me wrapped around her finger and she knew it. I was going to have to tell her that she needed to find some help other than me sooner rather than later but I wasn't eager to kick her out again. She had a habit of leaving and getting herself into even worse trouble like the other night when I'd rescued her from Tippy's. Thankfully she hadn't been high but she was so drunk she could barely walk. I had exchanged a few choice words to the bartender before leaving. His job was to serve alcohol but it was also to protect his patrons and make sure they didn't die from alcohol poisoning.

"Who is Stacy?"

I turned around and shrugged my shoulders. "Some girl I know." That was a lie. She wasn't just some girl. She was the girl I wanted to spend more time with and get to know better. She was the girl who could brighten my day no matter how shitty I was feeling. I sighed heavily. "She's a girl I want to know better. What did she say?"

"Not much. She sounded surprised that I was on the other end. Didn't you tell her about me?"

"No," I growled as I rubbed the back of my neck in frustration. I wanted to punch something. Who knew what was going on in Stacy's mind? I hadn't called her after our kiss and near oral on her bed. I was an asshole. "I need to call her back."

"Yeah, you should. I'm glad you have someone, Rio, I was starting to think you were going to live here all alone forever. We both know what happened to Penny was shitty but we both also know that it wasn't your fault. I share in the blame just as much as you do and there wasn't much I could've done to stop it from happening either."

I clenched my jaw and started to walk away. I didn't want to talk about her.

"Rio, you can't keep running from it. You have to face it. Just as much as I do. Why do you think I'm still using? I can't forget finding her. That memory of her is burned into my brain. And I can't help but think that if I'd just been sober enough to drive that I could've gotten there before it was too late. Before..."

I turned and stared at her. "Don't. You weren't responsible for her. You weren't her blood. I was."

"And you weren't responsible either. You weren't her father."

Just the mention of him caused my insides to tighten to an uncomfortable level. "But I should have been there. I was her big brother. That's what they do. That's why girls have big brothers so they can save them from fucked up shit."

"No, Rio, that's a hero. That's a knight in shining fucking armor, and you are not a knight. You're a man."

"And you're an addict."

"Takes one to know one."

She had me there. "True. And you know that the right thing for you to do is to check yourself into rehab and get some help. If you don't you're just going to end up in the same damn place."

"Yours. Is that so bad, really?"

"Yes. You need to clean yourself up and live, Annie."

"This is living. Being fucked up and high as shit is the epitome of living! I never feel so good as when I'm high. I can forget everything and just be...free! Carpe diem!"

"No. That's dying. That is letting your addiction own you. Own yourself, Annie. Finally. You are free from it. Free from your mother and high school and our shit-ass little hometown. You're free from it all. Do something that you've always wanted to do. Live!"

I watched her expression as I slowly tore down her walls. And then I watched as they quickly went back up. "I'm not ready. Okay? I'm not ready." She pushed past me and out the door into the freezing night air. My jaw ached as I decided whether or not I should go after her. I shook my head and went back into my bedroom to change the sheets. They still smelled like the vomit she'd laid on them when she was coming down from her drunken escapade.

Once the sheets were cleaned and the window was cracked open to get rid of the smell I went to the kitchen. My stomach was growling as I stared into the empty fridge. I sighed and slammed the door shut. Right. I was going to call for fucking pizza when Annie had distracted me. I slipped into my jacket and headed out. After a few slices of pizza I'd be a new man. And maybe Annie would be home and thinking logically by then and I could work at being a little closer to helping her kick her addiction.

Stacy

It felt a little strange being at the bar alone, knowing that I was going to remain alone until some man came over and tried to pick me up. I licked my lips as I sat down at an empty barstool. I was already regretting my rash clothing decision. I felt naked and exposed and slutty.

I kept my eyes straight ahead as the bartender, a female dressed in a wife beater and ripped jeans, came over. She was about a decade older than me with her hair up in a ponytail. It curled and hung down in ringlets that reminded me of the cheerleaders in my high school. I cleared my throat and smiled. "Hi. Can I get a beer?"

"Tap or bottle? House beer is on special right now."

"Um, I'll take the special, thanks."

I'd handed over my credit card and sat back, my eyes on a basketball game I had no interest in. After I'd finished off my beer I moved on to mixed drinks. It took a while before a man came up next to me at the bar and wrapped his arm around my shoulders. His arm felt warm but it didn't give me butterflies. Unlike with Rio. I turned to face the nice smelling guy. I had to get my mind off of Rio. That's why I was here, I reminded myself. I stared up into his handsome face. His dark eyes were studying me, his smile deepened when he got a good look at my face.

"A beautiful face to match that rocking body. It's my lucky night."

"Maybe," I said with a smirk.

"Maybe? Aww, come on, sweetheart. All you can give me is a little hope?"

I shrugged, a smile still on my lips. Flirting was one of my strengths. "A little hope could take you a long way, if you're lucky. What's your name?"

"Nolan."

"What are you doing out so late on a school night, Nolan?"

He grinned, "Why do you ask? You going to tell my mommy?"

I shook my head, which felt like it was filled with air. I'd already had quite a few drinks. "Not unless you're a very, very bad boy."

He pushed some of my hair aside and then leaned down and whispered into my ear. "I bet you won't tell her even if I was a very, very bad boy. Something tells me you like your men bad."

"What makes you say that?" I asked, my heart rate skyrocketing.

"I just can't see some pansy-ass preppy boy ramming himself into you and making you scream out the way I know I could."

Darkness danced in my vision and I felt like I was going to hit the floor. I grabbed onto the bar even as his arm steadied me. I crawled off the stool and murmured something about the bathroom and pulled my phone from my pocket. As my free hand pushed on the door I looked over my shoulder at him and his eyes seemed to be laughing at me. Had he done something? Or did he just think I was amusing? I was holding onto anything I could as my vision continued to pulse. My bleary-eyed stare in the mirror was the last thing I saw before the blackness.

Chapter 18

Rio

My phone rang as I stepped out of the pizza place. I'd decided to eat there and bring home the leftovers. I looked at the phone and quickly flipped it open when I saw Stacy's name. "Hey, I'm so sorry that I haven't returned your call yet." I paused and waited for her response. I put the leftovers into my backpack. Maybe she was still mad at me. "I'm an asshole, Stacy. I'm sorry." I stood beside my bike and really listened. The feeling of discord was forming a thick knot in my chest as I listened to the eerie silence, the faint loud thumping of music, and general crowd noise that was playing in the background of where-ever she was. "Stacy? Stacy?!" I felt so helpless in that moment. I waited. I wasn't going to hang up first. I listened. There was some laughter, classic rock music, but nothing that gave away where she might be. Except that it was a probably a bar.

There were lots of choices but only a few that were close to the college. I could only hope that she'd gone to one of those otherwise I'd be searching all night. I got into my van and started to drive in that direction, the phone still pressed to my ear. After a moment I heard a female gasp and then some hollow footsteps.

"HELLO?" I shouted as loud as I could into the phone, causing my own eardrums to ring. I waited a moment and listened again. There was some more shuffling and I still didn't hear a voice. Damnit.

I was almost there. Stacy just had to hang in there a little longer. I hoped someone was busy calling 9-1-1. As I turned down Main Street I found parking for the first bar, McGilly's Pub. I hopped off my bike, phone still pressed to my ear and stepped inside. There was an Irish band playing. This wasn't it. I turned around and stepped up to my bike. I was about to throw my leg over when I heard some voices close by.

"Oh shit! What do we do?"

"I don't know! That's why I got you, I thought you would know!"

"HELLO?" I shouted again, hoping to get the hysterical drunk girls' attention.

"Did you hear that?"

I sighed to myself. "PICK UP THE PHONE!"

There was some clattering and then the female voice was loud and in my ear. Finally. "Hello?"

"Thank God. Where is she? What bar are you in? I'm coming to get her."

"We're at Vinnie's on Vine."

Fuck. That was at least twenty minutes away. "I need you to hang up with me and call 9-1-1. Can you do that?"

"Y-yeah. I can do that."

"Good. Do it."

I hung up the phone and shoved it into my pocket before riding like a bat out of hell to get my ass across town. I didn't want to miss the ambulance when they took her. If I did I probably wouldn't know which hospital they'd taken her to and that would be another battle I'd have to face. The panic in my chest started to clutch me tightly and I heard my heart pounding in my ears. I hoped she was okay.

***

I was almost sideswiped by a car but I'd made it to Vinnie's in time to see Stacy's face before the EMT technicians closed the doors.

"Fuck!" Like a lawyer desperate for a client, I tailed the ambulance all the way to Memorial. I quickly parked and ran to the ER. I wasn't the fittest of guys, I preferred lifting weights to running, so I was out of breath by the time I reached the ER desk.

"Hi. I'm looking for my friend. She was just brought in. Stacy…"

The nurse must have seen the wild recognition in my eyes that I had no fucking clue what her last name was because she immediately pointed to the waiting area. I glanced behind me and stared at all the people sitting, waiting for their turn, masks and throw up bags included.

With a defeated sigh I pointed to the wall of the waiting room across from her desk questioningly. She nodded and I went that way. I crossed my arms over my chest as I struggled to figure out what I could do to see her. I wanted to know that she was okay. But I wasn't going to get in there without being immediate family or whatever fucked up rules they had. I was about to dial Elly to ask her about Stacy's last name but my phone started to ring. I answered the unknown number with a slight growl. "Hello?"

"Hi. Rio? This is Dr. Higgins at Memorial Hospital. I have someone you know here."

I felt my heart skip a beat and breathed a sigh of relief. "Oh thank God. You have Stacy?"

"Uh, no. We have Annie Pike. She has you listed as her Emergency Contact."

My heart skipped another beat and then calmed. She probably OD'ed or had alcohol poisoning. "Is she alright?"

"You need to come to the hospital so we can talk."

"Talk about what? Is she alright or not?"

"Please come see me in the Emergency Department. You can ask the front nurse for me and she'll escort you back."

I hung up the phone and stomped back into the ER. The nurse looked a little annoyed as I approached again, but she was cordial.

"Yes? How can I help you?"

"I just got a call from Dr. Higgins. He said my friend, Annie Pike, is back there and that he needs to talk to me."

She nodded and then picked up the phone, "One moment."

After speaking with who I could only presume was the doctor she hung up the phone and then stood up behind the desk. She moved towards the "Do Not Enter" door and held her pass in front of it. The door moved open and she motioned for me to go inside.

"Dr. Higgins will meet you at the desk in a moment."

The area behind the doors was clean and most of the bays for patients had their curtains closed. My palms itched a little to take a peek, I wanted to see Stacy and I was pretty sure she was in here somewhere. I clenched my jaw tightly and went to the ER nurse's desk, as instructed, and waited for the pretty blonde nurse behind the counter to acknowledge me.

"Hi. You must be Rio Levant, Ms. Pike's emergency contact?"

"Yeah."

"Does she have any family we could call for her?"

"Uh... no. She doesn't keep in contact with her mom anymore. They're estranged."

The nurse nodded and then licked her lips. "Alright, well, just wait right here and I'll snag Dr. Higgins when he's finished with his current patient.

I nodded and glanced around. There wasn't much to see but there was plenty to hear. The beeping of machines, the whirring of the heat blowing into the large room from several vents on the ceiling. Moans and cries from people in pain. I shifted and tried to ignore it. The sound of people suffering deeply disturbed me, I'd heard lots of suffering after my mother had died from the injuries she's sustained in her car accident and I didn't like to think of it.

I cleared my throat and glanced up just in time to see an older man leaving one of the patient bays. I caught a glimpse of the man behind the curtain. I was disappointed that it wasn't Stacy.

"Dr. Higgins, Ms. Pike's EC is here." The nurse had stood up and motioned to me. The doctor nodded and then handed a file over to the nurse.

"Get those into the computer. I also need to order an extra for Bay Three."

She nodded and did as he requested as he turned to me. The look on his face went from one of concentration to one of discomfort. His discomfort was rubbing off on me and I shifted again.

"Jesus Christ. Just tell me."

"Ms. Pike came in about an hour ago. She'd been hit by a car while she was crossing the street. We did everything that we could but..."

I didn't hear the rest of what he said. The finality of what he was saying had already registered in my mind. Annie was dead. I put my fists in my hair and pulled on it, trying to make myself come back to reality. I didn't want to be in my head. I tried to remember the last thing I'd said to her before she'd walked out of my house. Had I been kind? Her last words echoed in my mind.

I'm not ready to live, okay? I'm not ready.

I didn't want to hear them. They would haunt me for days, months, maybe even years. If I'd gone after her, stopped her, been nicer, she wouldn't have been outside. She wouldn't have been crossing that street. She would still be alive.

The doctor's hand on my shoulder caused me to snap out of my brain. His face was blurry, the discomfort from earlier had changed to concern.

"Just come sit down here for a minute, son. I know that was a lot to process."

With a firm hand he guided me towards an empty chair that I hadn't noticed was set off in the corner. I wondered how many other people had sat in this chair to collect themselves after just being told that someone they knew had died.

He gave my shoulder a couple more pats and then walked away again to talk to the nurse. My eyes started to wander and the walls felt like they were caving in around me. Everything was a morbid hospital blue. The same blue that I had seen when I was with my mother when she'd died. The same blue that I had seen every time I woke up in a hospital bed after my father had railed on me or after I'd had too much to drink and gotten into a fight with him that I couldn't win. There'd been too many times to count.

I inhaled deeply and stood up. I was heading for the exit when the doctor entered another patient's section. My breath caught in my chest as I caught just a glimpse. Stacy's beautiful face was pale. Like a moth drawn to a flame I went to her. The doctor wasn't paying much attention as he wrote down a few notes after checking her lifeless eyes.

"Is she dead too?"

He looked up at me and frowned.

"Do you know her too?"

I nodded. "Is she dead?"

He sighed as he stuffed his pen into his white coat pocket. "No, she's not dead. She was drugged and fell on the tile floor. She has a mild concussion but it's probably nothing serious. She'll most likely be fine and have a headache for a few days. She isn't going anywhere tonight. Go home, Mr. Levant. Stacy is in good hands."

I blinked as he reached up and pulled the curtain in place, shutting me out. It was where I deserved to be. Shut out. I apparently couldn't love without the final outcome being death. Love? Fuck. I did. I loved her.

Stacy

I groaned as I came back to the real world. My head was aching. I tried to reach up to rub it but my hand was stuck on something. I gasped in pain as I tried to pull it free and the needle started to rip from my skin. "Oh shit." I glanced around, trying to figure out where I was, what had happened. I was in the hospital. I tried to recount the events that had led to me getting here but the last thing I'd remembered was my reflection in the mirror and that guy smiling at me. Fuck. The pain in my head and now my arm was pulling me from my sleepy state. I glanced around for someone to help me and found a red call button instead. After a minute of me holding my IV in place the nurse finally came in. She frowned at me as she came over to assess the damage.

"I didn't know it was there and I pulled."

"I'll say. We're going to have to IV your other hand and bandage this one up."

I nodded and closed my eyes. "What happened to me?"

The nurse's eyes glanced at me every few seconds as she spoke and went about fixing me up. "You were drugged and were lucky enough to have fallen in public. Does your head hurt?"

"Yeah," I managed to get out. My throat felt like sandpaper. "How long have I been here?"

"You came into the ER last night and you were brought up here this morning."

"Does anyone know I'm here?"

"We called your mother last night. She said she was coming this afternoon."

I nodded and felt some of the panic wash away. My mom was coming. That was something.

"Thank you," I said as I looked at the bandage. It was a double meaning. I looked at the other arm and watched carefully as she stuck another needle into my vein. I winced a little but held still for fear that she'd have to stick me again. Once the initial pain subsided my mind raced to catch up. It was Thursday and I wasn't in class. I'd need to tell my professors somehow about my hospital stay.

"Can I call someone?"

She checked the IV bag and then stared down at me. "You can, but you should try to rest. You don't need any outside stress. You need to heal."

"Do you have my phone?" I asked, I wasn't going to back down and she knew it. She grabbed my purse and set it on the tray. She pushed it to the side of my bed. "Thanks," I said again.

"You're welcome. Let me know if you need anything else. You know how the button works." She smiled a little and then left me alone.

I rifled through my purse with my bandaged hand because I didn't want to risk messing up another IV. I found my phone in there and pulled it out. My battery was running really low so I probably only had enough juice to call one person. Elly or Rio? Not Rio. He was probably still with that girl. I dialed Elly and put the phone to my ear.

"Hey Stacy, what's up?"

"Hey. Not much, just sitting in a hospital bed."

"What?"

"Yeah. Thought I could use a vacation."

"Shut up! What happened??"

"I blacked out. The nurse said someone slipped something in my drink and I blacked out on the floor."

"Oh my god. Was anyone with you?"

"No. But lesson learned. Do not go to the bar alone. Men will drug you."

"Oh my god. Are you okay?"

"I have a headache and I accidentally mangled my hand but I'm okay. What are you up to today?"

"We have band practice right after lunch. Do you want me to come by and see you? Bring you something?"

"No. That's okay. My mom will be here soon. Oh, do you think you could email Professors Smith and Klein and let them know that I won't be in class today.'"

"Of course. I'm sorry I didn't go with you. I feel like a huge jerk right now, I was just-"

My phone beeped once and then died. I sighed. I put my phone away as my head sank back into my pillow. The nurse wasn't kidding. I was exhausted. The steady sound of the beeping was all I heard before I fell back asleep.

Chapter 19

Rio

There was loud banging on my front door. I groaned as I rolled over, the tinkling of beer bottles sounded as I stepped out of the pile of them. "I'm coming!" Why did they have to bang on my fucking door so fucking loudly? I opened the door and winced as the afternoon sun pierced my eyes. I shaded them with a hand.

"What the fuck happened to you?" I couldn't see his face because of that fucking sun but I knew his voice.

"Nice to see you too," I muttered as I left the front door and moved to my bedroom. "What the fuck do you want, James?"

"I want to practice and so does the rest of the band who is going to be here in less than an hour."

Fuck, he was following me. Why couldn't he take a fucking hint?

"Call them. We're cancelling. Cancelling everything."

"The fuck we are, dude. I need this money. Get your drunk ass in the shower and sober up." He moved past me into my bathroom and turned on the shower.

"Fuck off. I'm going to go back to sleep."

"It's going to be real fucking hard to sleep with live rock music shaking your house, dude."

I ignored him and was almost to my bed when hands grabbed onto my shirt and pushed me into the bathroom. I caught myself against the wall, barely, and turned around.

"That was fucked up, James! I could've fucking hurt myself!"

"You already did hurt yourself, dumbass. Get in the shower. It makes me sick to think about it but I'll fucking undress you if I have to."

I struggled to pull off my shirt but the rest was pretty easy. My sweatpants and boxers just slipped right off and into the shower I went. My body was shocked at the frigid temperature which had taken a moment to register. "AH! Fuck!" I shoved the faucet dial with my foot and slowly the temperature started to rise and then it started to boil. "AHHH! Fuck!!" I turned it the other way with my foot and then hunched myself in the corner of the shower. I tested the temperature with my foot and once it was stable I inched myself back in and then adjusted it from there.

The cold and hot had unfogged my brain just enough for the memories to come back.

I'm not ready to live, okay? I'm not ready.

She'd been hit by a car while she was crossing the street. We did everything that we could but...

Go home, Mr. Levant. Stacy is in good hands.

I rubbed at my eyeballs with the heels of my hands, trying to press out the tears that were starting to come. I needed another beer. Maybe some whiskey. Whiskey in the shower would be really fucking good. Whiskey would take away the pain that was threatening to swallow me whole.

I wasn't in the shower long, I was already feeling the hangover and that meant I was coming off the alcohol. I needed some more. James was sitting on my bed. He held out a glass of water, concern on his face. I ignored the water as I dropped my towel and got dressed. James grunted in disgust.

"You can try to scare me away with your balls all you want to but it isn't going to work. I'm going to get to the bottom of this relapse. Did something happen with Stacy?"

I pulled on some boxers and pulled my hair back, it was still drenched and dripping down my back. "Annie was hit by a car."

"...Fuck." While James was silent I pulled on the rest of my clothes, taking my time with it because I didn't want to face him.

"She was hit by a fucking car and now she's dead. Just like my sister. And it's my fucking fault."

James sat on the bed a moment longer while I shuffled down the hallway. The feelings were starting to come back and I wanted to numb them. I needed to numb them. I opened the fridge and stared into the emptiness. I slammed the door shut and stood up, shuffling back to my bedroom. I needed to go get more.

James was in the doorway, his hands facing outwards, blocking me. "Did you hit her with your car?"

I frowned at him.

"Did you push her in front of the car?"

My scowl deepened and if he didn't shut the fuck up I was going to make him by laying my fist into his fucking face.

"I didn't think so. So this isn't your fault. We need to get you to a meeting."

The thought of a meeting made my stomach churn and a cold sweat to break out on my forehead. I didn't want to face anyone, especially a room full of people who thought they knew what I was going through. They didn't. They had no fucking clue. "I'm not going to a stupid fucking meeting. It's not going to make me feel better. It's not going to bring her back. It's a waste of fucking time. Just let me handle this my own fucking way and then I'll be fine." I turned on my heel and headed for the door.

"Rio, where are you going, man?"

"To get a fucking kitten."

Stacy

The second time I woke my mother was staring down at me. Her large hazel eyes were filled with unshed tears and she was stroking the inside of my palm which was cradled in both her hands.

"Hey baby," she said softly, sitting up taller in her plastic chair.

"Hey mom." I shifted in my bed with a groan, the pain that was in my head was significantly less than before. Things were already looking up. "Sorry to drag you out here."

"No, it's been too long since I've come to visit you. I'm going to come visit more often."

"Well, pretty soon you won't need to. I'm going to come back home after I get my degree."

"Stacy, you don't want to live in Jonesboro. For one, you hated it there. You always talk about how much you hate it. Up until this year you kept trying to get me to move away. And for another thing, you'll never find a decent husband there."

As much as I didn't want to bring Hank into this or even use his name in conjunction with the word husband, I needed to prove a point. I'd been hurt and alone and by the grace of strangers I was saved. But I didn't want to be surrounded by strangers. I wanted my mama.

"You did. You found more than one husband there."

Her eyes were staring at our hands, I couldn't see what my words had done to her. When she spoke her voice was soft. "That's true, Stacy, but I want better for you than I had. That's why you're in college and you're going to get a degree. And I can't let you come back to Jonesboro. I want better for you."

I felt a twinge in my heart at her words. How could she love me so much and not see what I saw when I looked at her? She was a good woman, the best mama, and she deserved better too. "Mama, I want better for you too. You're still beautiful inside and out despite what's happened to you. You can still be happy." I gently squeezed her hand.

She inhaled sharply as she looked up and away, the tears glistening there in her eyes. "Stacy." It was her warning tone, the one that she always used when I was doing something to upset her. But I wasn't going to stop now. She needed to hear it.

"Mama. I know you don't like to hear it unless it's from a man but you're beautiful and kind and fun. You're wasting yourself on Hank and Jonesboro."

Her hands tightened around mine as she shook her head, her tears growing fuller, on the verge of spilling over.

"You took care of me and when I get my degree I won't mind taking care of you too. You can live with me until you have enough saved from your new job to move out on your own."

She continued to shake her head. I could only hope that my words were getting through to her. I meant them. Every last bit of them. I wanted to help her get out of this life she couldn't seem to escape from. She blinked rapidly for a few seconds, her tears finally falling down her high cheekbones. She brusquely brushed them away before meeting my eyes. Her nose was red at the just the tip, mine looked the same whenever I cried.

"Alright, Stacy. I'll think about it."

I squeezed her hand tighter and nodded, relief flooding me, hope radiating my insides and shining through in a small smile. "Thank you." The sound of footsteps took my attention away from my mama.

The nurse was standing near the doorway, a strained smile on her thin lips. "Sorry to bother you but there is a man here. And he wants to see you. He's causing quite a stir and if you don't want to see him I'll call security for you."

I sat up a little taller and pushed my hair away from my face. A man? Who could it be? Was it the guy from the bar who drugged me? Because I sure wouldn't mind seeing him and calling the cops to arrest him for trying to date rape me. Or was it Rio? Had he found out what happened? The thumping in my chest was telling me it knew exactly who I was hoping it would be.

"You can let him in, I guess."

The nurse nodded and left the room. We could see her waving from the doorway and then a moment later Rio was standing in the doorway.

His blue eyes had circles so dark under them I was wondering if he'd been sleep deprived or punched. His hair, normally pulled back at the base of his head was scraggly and sticking up from his head in every direction. He was wearing a pair of gray sweatpants and a stained college hoodie. In short, he looked like shit.

"Rio?"

His eyes seemed to light up when they fixed on me but the moment was short lived as his gaze traveled to my mother who stood up protectively in front of me. She put her hands up and shook her head.

"Oh no, young man. I don't think so."

He frowned, his body swaying slightly. His jaw clenched tightly along with his fists at his side. "I do think so. I think so very much," his words not quite clear.

It was my turn to frown. What the hell was wrong with him?

"You're not going to come in here and see my daughter while you're shit-faced. Go home and sober up and then you can come back."

"No. I can't go home. He's there."

"Who is there?" I asked but my mom shushed me.

"I don't care if the devil himself is taking a shit in your toilet at home. You. Will. Not. Stay. Here. Go!"

There was a long quiet moment when they stared at each other. Rio's eyes clashed with my mama's. I saw his face slowly change from one of determination to one of remorse. Rio turned around, looking like a dog who'd just had the crap beaten out of him, and walked back out the door. There was nothing I wanted more at that moment than to get up out of my hospital bed and go after him so that I could offer him some comfort.

My mama faced me and shook her head. "You know nothing about good choices, do you, Stacy?"

"Rio? Mom, come on. First of all, I'm not with Rio. We are just friends." She huffed but I ignored her. "Second of all, even if we were more than that he isn't a terrible guy. Mostly. He's a human being and he has his faults, sure, but he's not a monster. Not like–"

"Don't say it."

I smiled to my mother innocently and shrugged my shoulders. "Okay, I won't." We stared at each other for a long moment before she turned around.

"I'm going to see when you're allowed to be released. I'll be right back."

I sighed and put my head back as I watched her leave my room. I turned my head to look out the window. Slowly the sun was starting to fall from the middle of the sky. I turned my head to see if it was still afternoon. As I stared my mind shifted to Rio and what he'd said. Who was there at his house? What was he running from? I was wondering if I'd ever find out when I heard footsteps in my doorway and turned my attention back there, expecting to see my mother in the doorway.

"That was–" but my words were cut off because Rio was standing there, his ice blue eyes locked onto me, causing my heart to beat wildly in my chest. I swallowed back some embarrassment as the heart monitor exposed my internal signals. Luckily for me he was apparently too drunk to notice. He came and sat down in my mom's chair and when he kissed my hand I could smell the beer on his breath. He was drunk, sure enough. "What's wrong?" I sat up straighter and covered my hand with his.

He shook his head, not meeting my eyes. "I'm just an asshole, Stacy. That's all."

Oh god. Had he slept with that Annie girl? Did he come here to tell me off for good? I tried to push those feelings away, it wasn't even like we were together. Not really. We had a few good moments and that was all.

His forehead touched the back of my hand and I winced, the area was still very sore from the ripped flesh. He put his head up after a delayed second and looked at my hand.

"What happened? Did-did you punch someone?" He was thumbing my hand with enough force that it hurt so I pulled it away and put it into my lap.

"No, it was an accident."

"You accidentally punched someone?"

"No. Are you going to tell me what happened to you?"

His eyes dropped again.

"My mama is going to be back soon so you'd better get to talking, Rio. What the hell happened to you?"

His large hand reached out and touched my leg. He was shaking. Not visibly but when he touched me I could feel the tremor. I put my hand on top of his.

"She's gone."

"Who?"

"Annie. She's gone."

The twinge of jealousy twisted deep in my chest. I had no right to feel it, I knew, but it didn't matter. All I could think of was Rio and Annie, whoever she was, tangled together in his sheets. I could see him rejoicing at having her and then losing himself in the bottle when she left him.

"What do you want from me, Rio? A quick fuck to make you feel better? Has she done this before? Is that what happened that night at the bar? You were looking for someone to fill the hole that Annie left in your heart?"

His eyes shot up to meet mine, unshed tears were lingering there. I tried to study his face but that was shot to shit when he sprung from the chair and headed for the door.

"I'm glad you're okay, Stacy. But that was a fucked up thing to say."

And without another word he left. I heard my mother shouting at him in the hallway and then she reappeared. She stared at me from the doorway, her eyes taking me in. I was stunned, not sure what had just happened.

"Did he hurt you?"

Just my heart. But I was pretty sure that wasn't what she was talking about. I shook my head. "No, mom."

Chapter 20

Rio

I went to her for solace, for comfort, and she fucking accuses me of wanting to use her. I grabbed onto my hair and pulled. I didn't want to think right now. It had been a mistake to go there and see her. I had to make sure she was breathing and conscious. I was lying to myself. I had needed to see her. Before she'd said the fucked up thing she had said I felt better while I was there with her. She soothed me. Just being with her was more of a relief than the alcohol induced state I'd been living in for the past twelve hours.

I grabbed a cab and slouched in the dirty back seat of it. My eyes met the cab driver's and something about them were familiar.

"Where to?" he asked, his eyes dancing between myself and the road in front of him as he pulled out into traffic.

"The liquor store and then I'm going home."

He nodded and then turned his full attention back to the road. The radio was abuzz with voices, discussing politics and the news. I tried to drown it out. The car lurched to a stop and I got out. "Keep the meter running, I'll be right back."

After grabbing myself two bottles of Jack and a six-pack of Coke I made my way back into the cab.

"258 Martin Street, right?"

I frowned at him. "Yeah, how the hell did you know that?" This was some freaky shit. Did he pickpocket me from the front seat? My mind was trying to figure out how he'd pull that off when he answered me.

"I drove you home a couple months ago. You had a pretty girl with you."

Fuck. I looked around on the backseat, wondering if there would be some trace of her there. I put my hand on the spot where her ass had been and I caressed it. Maybe if I closed my eyes and tried really hard I could pretend I was caressing her.

"You break up?"

I pulled my hand away and shook my head. "We just fucked."

His eyebrows shot up and he nodded his head, turning his full attention back to the road. I chuckled. Like he hadn't heard vulgar language before. Or maybe he saw through me. Maybe he knew that I was talking out of my ass. We didn't just fuck. It was more than that. Or it had been. And that brought me back to the present. Annie was dead. Stacy thought Annie had been my girlfriend.

The cab dropped me off at my place and almost immediately I wanted to turn around and call him back. Waiting for me was the band. All of them. Sitting outside in the cold looking like a pitiful intervention. I held tightly onto my bottle of Jack and my six pack of Coke. They weren't going to wrestle it away from me. It was mine. And if I ever deserved to let go and lose myself it was now.

They were as silent as ghosts as I stepped between them and into my house. And like ghosts who were waiting for someone to freak the fuck out, they followed me. I ignored them and went into the kitchen and made myself a drink. After I'd thrown back half of it I looked up. Big mistake.

I could see the pity in all of their faces. James, the big mouth, had probably told the other two all of my fucking business.

"Don't fucking look at me like that. I'm dealing with my shit."

"You're trying to drown your shit," Elly said.

I scoffed. "Like you're one to talk. You drowned your shit a few weeks ago. And I bet you cry every night and every morning. And you're on the verge of doing it fucking now. Elly, he didn't fucking want you."

James started to yell at me as Elly turned away and rushed outside. I took another drink, watching her go. She was better off without that tool and she was better off running away from me. And then a flash of the other night came into my head and I slammed my drink down and pushed past James who was still yelling about something and followed after her.

She was halfway down the street by the time I caught up. I grabbed her and spun her around to face me. She was crying. "Don't. Don't walk home."

She tried to pull away from me but I wanted her to agree. I couldn't let her go away upset like Annie had. I couldn't let her make the same mistake. If something happened to her on my watch...I don't know what I'd do.

"What the fuck do you care what I do?" I closed my eyes tightly and tried to will some humanity back into myself. "I care, Elly. I do. I'm just hurting. I fucked up. Again. I fucked up really bad and there are no do-overs or second chances."

She hugged me. I was taken aback. I'd been a complete asshole to her and she was hugging me.

"Elly, I'm not looking to be your rebound."

Elly didn't say anything, she just held onto me tighter. I put my arms around her and hugged her too. When I closed my eyes I could imagine it was my sister. She had been tiny, like Elly. For a moment I thought it was her.

"I'm so sorry," I whispered. "I'm so sorry I wasn't there to save you from him. From yourself." I was talking about my dad, but she didn't know that. And she didn't care. And neither did I. I was so fucked up.

"But I'm here to save you from yourself. We all are. Don't go down that path, Rio. Pour it out and sleep it off."

"I can't," I said, the words barely able to leave my lips. "I can't get rid of it. It's all I have. It's the only thing I have left."

"No," she said. When she pulled back she looked into my eyes. I felt the churning grow in my guts. "You have all of us. You have your band. You have your house and your future. Don't drink that away. Alcohol isn't worth it. It's just a quick fix."

I squeezed my eyes closed. I knew she was right. I knew alcohol wasn't the answer but it did make things bearable, livable.

I was released from the hospital the following morning and was driven by my mom to my apartment just after. I spent the day tidying up my apartment and studying. I'd missed two days of classes and desperately needed to catch up. Later that evening I was heating up something to eat for dinner when my cell started to ring.

"Hello?"

"Stacy? Thank God. I've been trying to call you for hours. I was just about to call a cab to go to the hospital to see if you were still there." Elly's voice was slightly panicked, which wasn't usually like her.

I felt my anxiety level rise as I moved towards the window to look outside. I needed to look at something to help preserve my composure and be strong for her. "Is something wrong? Is it Kent?"

"No, it's not Kent. It's Rio. He's... he's on a bender. And I've known him as long as you have but I'm worried about him. And from what I've heard from James this is really bad."

I felt relief in my chest all at once. "What's bad? Him drinking himself into a stupor? He's a human and he's upset about this Annie person being gone. It's only natural that he'd drown his sorrows in a bottle." And a ho. I didn't say it, but I was thinking it and the thought of Rio rolling around with some girl made that horrible jealousy rear its ugly head again.

"No. Stacy, he's a recovering alcoholic."

The microwave dinged in the background and there was a moment when my heart stopped beating in my chest. A recovering alcoholic? How did I not know that? "I don't understand. If he's a recovering alcoholic what was he doing in the bar that night we met? Wh–" I paused and scoffed. My mind was reeling as I tried to piece everything together.

"He's been sober for a couple of years, I guess he thought he could handle it. But that was before Annie was killed."

My heart did it again and suddenly I felt like the biggest bitch on all seven continents. "She's dead?"

"Yes. She was over here and they had some disagreement and then she left. When she was crossing the street she was hit by a car and ... she didn't recover."

"Oh God."

"We tried to get through to him but he just kicked us all out of his house. I'm worried about him, Stacy, anddoorbelldoorbell I know you two aren't an official thing but... it would be worth a try for you to go over there, wouldn't it?"

My mind was reeling. Was she asking me to do something?

"Go over where?"

"Stacy! Go to Rio's house. See if you can get through to him. He needs someone to save him from himself."

I couldn't believe that either. Not for a second. He was so capable. So protective of others. So strong. But he hadn't been so strong when he'd walked into the hospital. He'd shown his weakness to me when he touched my leg. He had been asking for comfort and I'd pushed him away with my insecurities. Regardless of whether or not Annie and Rio had something going on between them, she was dead now. And he clearly needed someone. And for whatever reason he'd chosen me. "I'll go. But I can't make any promises."

With a pizza in my hand I approached Rio's front door and rang the doorbell. It was getting really fucking hot on the underside of the box as the seconds ticked by. I knocked on the door, waited another few minutes and then tried the door. Locked. I knew he was in there. Both of his vehicles were parked in the driveway. I stepped off the porch and, like a stalker, started walking around the exterior of his house. I glanced in the windows and tried to see if I could spot him. Nothing. Maybe he'd gone for a walk somewhere. Maybe he was already so far gone that he was passed out. Maybe he'd choked on his own vomit.

Fear started to seize my chest and I set the pizza on one of his flat bushes and ripped off the screen. I tugged on the window. Locked. I ripped off the next screen and did the same. Locked. Fuck!

I stepped back to observe the lock and then quickly ran around his house, checking the locks. Bingo. The window around the back wasn't locked. I ripped off the screen and pushed the window open. "Rio?!"

Silence greeted me. I pushed the window open as far as it would go and squeezed myself into his bedroom. I landed on his floor with a dull thud but was quickly on my feet. I had to make sure he was all right.

"Rio?" I glanced around and listened. I heard the TV in the living room and running water. I stared at the closed bathroom door and approached it cautiously. Part of me was afraid of what I'd find behind the door. He wasn't suicidal, was he?

I turned the knob and slowly opened the door, peeking my head in as it cracked. I didn't see much but steam but I heard low sobs coming from the direction of the shower. I closed my eyes tightly as my heart clenched and broke for him. His sobbing ended abruptly, he must have heard me. I quickly knocked on the door, pretending I hadn't heard anything and then opened it loudly.

"Rio? It's me, Stacy. I brought you some dinner."

There was a moment's pause, only the sound of the water raining from the shower head, before he spoke. "Not hungry."

"Come on, grumpy pants. Come have dinner with me. I have something I want to tell you."

There was more silence between us as the shower turned off. I closed the door just before the shower curtain rings jangled across the metal bar. I heard hard foot falls as he made his way out of the shower. I quickly retreated to his bed, the backs of my knees hit it and I fell backwards.

I sat up just as he came out of his bathroom. A towel hanging low on his damp hips. I licked my lips as my curious eyes ran over his body. When I looked up I saw him staring at me. His eyes had dark circle all around him. It looked as if he'd been punched in both of them. His eyes glanced behind me to his window and I saw his neutral expression turn to one of confusion.

"What the fuck?" He staggered over and closed it, the chilly breeze no longer flowing through it.

"Oh, haha, I um, yeah. I had to climb through the window." I cleared my throat softly and watched the ripples of his back as he scrubbed his hands over his face.

"You broke into my house?" He turned to face me. He was standing there but his eyes were vacant. Or maybe just exhausted.

"I mean, not really. It was unlocked."

He raised an eyebrow and shook his head, he moved to his dresser and pulled out some boxers. He stepped into them after dropping his towel, giving me a few seconds to stare at his gorgeous ass.

I cleared my throat and moved towards the hallway. I needed to escape so that I could gather my thoughts. The man was grieving over another woman. I shouldn't have been thinking about molesting him. "Dinner is getting cold."

"How long have you been here?"

"Not long," I said, taking a tentative step behind him.

"It'll stay warm for a few more minutes," he said as he turned, his hand grasping me by my wrist, pulling me into his chest.

I bumped into him, my insides of my body instantly on fire. I pulled my hands back, trying so hard not to tempt myself. "No, it won't. It's still outside."

"Then fuck dinner. We can reheat it in the oven. After I've had you." He leaned down and tilted my chin up with his finger. His other hand was around my backside, curling against my lower back. He captured my lips with his.

And for a moment I was lost in him.

But once I tasted the whiskey I turned my face away and pushed back. He was mourning. He was trying to distract himself. "Rio, I'm not going to be your Band-Aid. If you want to talk, I'm here. But I'm not here to fuck you."

He held tight, his lips grazing over my neck, sending shivers through me. He knew what my traitorous body wanted. "I don't want you to fuck me, Stacy. I want to fuck you."

Despite his words, which literally melted me, I couldn't let him do this. He tried to kiss me again but I held firm and twisted out of his grip.

"Stop it."

He ran a hand through his still wet hair after he released me. "Fine. Stopped. Get out of my room."

I backed out of his room, his tone threatening, and dark with warning. I went outside and fetched the pizza. By the time I came back he was standing at the counter, pouring himself yet another drink. I bit my lower lip gently. Taking it from him was not going to go over well. I knew this from my years of experiences with many of my mother's exes, more than one had been an alcoholic.

I set the pizza on the counter and opened the box. I pulled out a slice and brought it to my lips. I was hungry. And maybe seeing me eat would tempt him into putting something in his stomach.

But he didn't look at me. He made his drink and walked right past me, into the living room.

Chapter 21

Rio

What the fuck was she doing here if she didn't want to distract me from my pain with sex? Pizza? Really? That wasn't going to make shit better. As much as I wanted to stand there and watch her use her mouth to tear into the pizza I knew it would just be torture, wishing she'd use her mouth in other capacities so that I could forget for a while.

She joined me in the living room and sat down on the couch beside me. I grunted, the heat of her body teasing me. I took a long pull from my glass, filling myself with fire that burned for a moment and then dulled everything.

"What the hell do you want, Stacy?"

"I just wanted to tell you that I'm sorry. About Annie. I didn't know that she'd..." she paused, hesitating, and obviously not wanting to try to set me off. She had no idea. "Is there anything I can do?"

I scoffed. "You can leave me alone. Or you can spread your legs." In my peripheral vision I saw her flinch at my words. I wondered how much more I'd have to say before she'd leave me alone. I didn't want her here if she wasn't going to distract me. My brain couldn't think of anything but sex when she was around. It was worse in its alcoholic pickled state.

"Neither of those are you going to happen. How about we talk?"

"How about we don't."

"How about we go sleep it off?"

I turned my head, looking at her expectantly. Sex? Did she mean sex? She shook her head and once again lost my attention.

"Nope. I'm watching a movie."

"Rio."

"Shh. I'm watching a movie."

She sighed and got up, moving to the kitchen. I wondered what she was doing in there but it didn't take long for me to find out. She'd grabbed more pizza, even took the time to put it on some plates and set one of them between us, presumably for me. I ignored it for now and drank some more.

We were quiet for a long time as the movie played on the TV. After she finished her pizza she got up and started moving around my house. I tried to ignore the clinking of glass as she cleaned up for me. I resented her for doing it. I was perfectly capable of taking care of myself. I pushed myself off the couch and went into the kitchen.

"What are you doing?"

She looked up at me, her face completely innocent, "I'm cleaning."

"No shit. Stop cleaning. This isn't your house."

She ignored me, dropping her head back to her task, and continued to pick up trash. I set my glass on the table and went over to her. I grabbed the trash bag from her and flung it off to the side. Glass shattered inside of it. Stacy's eyes followed it and then met mine.

"Stop," I repeated. I hoped my tone was firm enough that it scared her into submission. But I should have known better. Stacy was not submissive. She was strong. She didn't take shit.

She stepped over to the bag and picked it up again. "Go back to watching your movie, Rio."

I grabbed up my drink, refilled it and did exactly that. My head was starting to hurt from the frown on my brow but I continued to sit there, stewing. She was lucky that I didn't want to fight with her. She was lucky that I didn't have the ability to touch her without wanting to put her up against the nearest surface and sink into her.

I wanted her. I wanted her to distract me and take me away. The booze wasn't cutting it. Maybe I just wasn't drinking fast enough. I had a pretty decent tolerance, even after all these years away from it. It was like home. I threw it back and sank down further into the couch.

I heard the front door close and pretended I didn't care. If she left then good riddance. But I figured she was just taking out the trash. When the credits rolled on the movie I stood up and went to the front door. Did she leave me? I would deserve it. Unwanted tears pricked at my eyes, surprising me. Oh fuck, I was crying again like a little pussy. I opened the door a crack and saw her sitting on the front steps, phone pressed to her ear. I didn't want to admit that the sight of her had my eyes drying up. She hadn't left me. She was still here. And weirdly enough I felt safe.

I closed the door and went to the kitchen, grabbing the bottle of Jack before heading back to the couch. I turned my head when I heard some commotion at the window. I frowned as I watched Stacy try to put the screens back on my windows. What the fuck. She was ruining my house. She was a literal home wrecker.

I shook my head and looked back to the TV. As I stared my eyelids grew heavier and heavier. Sleep was coming for me and I was going to let it.

Stacy

I spent the rest of the evening half sitting, half lying beside the couch, my hand on Rio's. He slept soundly, which was impressive. I was fully expecting nightmares but they didn't come. Sometime after dawn, I felt him stir beneath my hand and I quickly moved it away, my eyes winced as the bright sunlight shone into the room.

I got up before he opened his eyes and moved to the bathroom. When I came out again I checked on him. He was still on the couch, his arm now slung over his eyes to block out the sun. I went into the kitchen and stared into his empty fridge. I sighed and shut the door. I grabbed his keys, donned my jacket, and drove myself to the store.

When I came back with my arms full of groceries I found Rio at the kitchen table, his head bent over the mostly empty bottle of Jack. I set the groceries down and put my hand on his shoulder. He shrugged it off violently and kept his eyes down.

"Okay." I was moving away from him when he reached out and grabbed my wrist. He pulled me back until I was sitting across his lap. He took my face in his warm hands and kissed me. It was desperate. He was seeking some physical comfort. I put my hands on his face and kissed him back, trying to ease him into something a little softer. He followed my lead and then his kisses faded as his emotions took over again.

"You should go, Stacy. Before I destroy you."

I ran my fingers through his hair, trying to soothe him. Even though I was still wondering if he'd destroyed Annie. I still wondered who she was to him. "You won't destroy me." This was a lie. He had the power to destroy me. He'd already partially crushed me and like a moth to a flame I was here with him. I couldn't leave him, not because Elly had asked but because I cared about this man.

He wrapped his arms around my waist, pulling me to him for a hug. I closed my eyes and relished the feeling. This was better. This was trust, comfort. Love? No. Rio didn't love me. He may have loved Annie. Would he drown himself in alcohol if I died? I wasn't sure.

"I'm a fucking mess," he murmured into my neck. I fought to keep ahold of my libido despite the raging war going on in my head.

"Yes, you are." He was quiet for a long time. I wondered what was going on in his head. I would've given almost anything to know. Was he thinking about Annie? Was he thinking about me?

"I'm going to have to leave for awhile to do my twelve steps. Elly is going to kill me," he said, his voice cracking with his pain. He was thinking about Elly and the band. And rehab. I swallowed back the disappointment I felt that he hadn't mentioned me in his list of names as I gently stroked his upper back.

"She won't. She just wants you to get better." I pressed a soft kiss to his forehead as I continued to move my hands over his back and hair. "We all just want you to get better."

He tilted his head back so he could look at me. I raised my eyebrows expectantly.

"I'm sorry. For everything."

There was so much in that statement. So much potential. What exactly was he sorry for? For using me? For not telling me about Annie? For showing up at the hospital? For drinking?

"I'm sorry too," I said. Because I was. I was sorry for saying the things I'd said to him about Annie. She'd obviously meant a lot to him.

He released a heavy sigh. "Can I have the raincheck for the cuddling now?"

I smiled and nodded my head. "Of course."

He set me on my feet and then joined me as we moved down the hallway to his bedroom. He pulled back the covers and slid in between them. He left plenty of room for me and, after I removed my shoes, I willingly climbed in with him. He spooned me, holding me tightly against his warm body.

"I can't believe that I failed again, Stacy."

I stroked the wrist that was across my stomach. "How did you fail?"

He was silent for a long time. When I turned around to see if he was still awake he nuzzled my neck with his nose and pulled me in closer to his body. His voice was a whisper. "First with Penny and now with Annie."

"Tell me about her?"

"Who?"

"Annie. Was she..." I tried to pull away, to distance myself so I could ready myself for the truth, but he held tight. "Was she your girlfriend or your lover? Did you two..."

"No," he said softly. "She was Penny's best friend."

"Penny is your sister."

"Was my sister. She OD'ed."

I let his words sink in for a moment. My hand went to his arm and I stroked him gently. "I'm sorry, Rio."

"It was a while ago. And I failed her. I failed them both. And I have to live with that. And that's why I drink. I don't want to live with that."

I turned in his arms and took his beautiful tortured face between my hands. I didn't know what to say to him. So I just held him.

He closed his eyes. "I haven't told anyone about Penny except the cops."

"You don't have to talk about it," I said because I could see that it was hurting him.

"No." He opened his eyes and stared into mine. My heart was melting all over again. "I want to tell you. I need to tell someone. She OD'ed because," he paused and I waited until he started again, "my son of a bitch father was hitting her. When I lived there he did it to me. And when I left I figured he'd stop or go find another man to hit. But he didn't. He was hitting her and she didn't tell me. She kept it from me. She suffered in silence. And she turned to drugs and alcohol to deal with his shit. And if I had been there, if I had come home once in a while I probably would've seen it. And I could've stopped it. I could've taken the pain for her." His voice was strangled in his throat.

My vision was blurry from my own tears. "It's not your fault. It's your dad's fault, Rio. It's his fault. It's a mark on his soul, not yours."

He turned his face to press a kiss to my palm and then whispered against it, "I wish that I knew. I wish that I'd gotten there before..."

"But you didn't. And that's not your fault." I wrapped my arms around him and hugged him tightly against me, trying to take all of his pain into myself. I didn't want him to suffer. I didn't want him to put this all on himself. He didn't deserve it. He hadn't done anything to deserve this. "It's over now, Rio. You have to forgive yourself. She would have forgiven you. I'm sure she knew that you loved her."

"She knew that I hated him. And I don't know if she knew that I loved her more than I hated him. I don't know if she knew I'd come rescue her."

"What ifs and wishes aren't going to get you anywhere except to the bottom of the bottle, Rio." I pressed a kiss to his neck and then to his cheek.

"I love you," he whispered, his hands tightened around me as his eyes met mine. We stared at each other for a long moment. I could feel the heat, the love moving between us. His eyes dropped to my lips and mine dropped to his as they parted and started to move towards mine.

His kiss was barely detectible. He was teasing me, testing me. Now that I knew he hadn't been with Annie and that I wasn't the woman on the side I could finally let him in. I gasped into his parted lips, the sound seemed to break through the tension between us and he claimed my lips fully, making me forget about anything else.

His hands moved over my body, undressing me with ease. I pulled at his shirt, pulling it over his head, my fingers raking his naked skin when it was finally exposed. He nipped at my neck and then moved lower, pushing me back onto my back. "Rio," I moaned, my voice sounding foreign to myself.

He didn't stop, he kept kissing me, kissing every inch of me. Savoring me. And I savored him and the way he was making me feel. The way he'd always made me felt.

I reached down between us, searching for his pants, wanting to free him so I could feel him inside of me. I wanted us to be together. He kneeled over me and undid his pants, pulling them off, letting them fall into a heap on the floor somewhere. He was stunning with the morning sunlight spilling across him. His skin golden and smooth, except for his chest which had just enough dark hair for me to sink my nails into.

My nipples perked at the coolness in the air. His hungry eyes drank in my body and then he lowered himself, kissing me again, making my blood boil.

My fingers moved through his hair, while I moaned and rolled as he caressed my body with his lips.

"Rio," I groaned.

I gasped as his fingers slipped between my folds, finding my sweet, wet spot.

It was his turn to groan as his fingers slid inside of me. "You're so wet," he said after popping my nipple from his mouth. He removed his hand and stroked himself with my wetness. So hot. He aligned himself and then balanced himself on one arm as he lowered his body and pressed himself inside of me.

We watched each other as our bodies melded together. My nails found his back, digging in as he stretched me to fit him. I rose and fell with him, our eyes only on each other as we made love.

Chapter 22

Rio

I groaned as I woke up fully, my eyes meeting with the harsh yellow light spilling out from the bathroom. The last thing I remembered was being buried deep inside Stacy. How that had happened, I didn't quite remember. The shower was running and there was steam spilling out of the bathroom. I closed my eyes to ease the ache in my head but the knocking that was coming from the front door was preventing my unconscious from taking over again. I lay there for a moment longer before forcing myself to get out of bed.

What had I done? I pulled on sweatpants before leaving my room and heading towards the door. The door swung open and James was standing there. He looked me over intently.

"Miss me?" I grunted as I shifted and leaned against the door jam and crossed my arms over my chest.

"You bet I did, cupcake. I just came to check on you and see how you were doing. Wanna go for a walk or something?"

I raised my eyebrow in disbelief. "A walk?" James casually shrugged his shoulders, his eyes dropped guiltily towards the ground, his hands shoved themselves into his jean pockets. "My head is killing me, man. I'm going to pack up my shit and make some phone calls and check into rehab. I'm taking care of it, okay?"

His eyes raked over my face, trying to judge my level of seriousness. I was deadly serious. I couldn't do this anymore. I didn't want to be this. I didn't want to wake up every morning feeling like I'd had my head run over by a semi-truck. This wasn't any way to live. When he realized I was serious he nodded and glanced behind him towards Stacy's car.

"So um...you and Stacy? Did you uh...?"

I closed my eyes tightly and shook my head. "That's really none of your fucking business, James. I appreciate you coming out here to check on me. Tell your dad I'm sorry that I'm not going to be coming to work for a couple of months but I need to get this taken care of."

James nodded. "Yeah, he'll understand. You work harder than four of his other workers put together. I'm sure you'll have a job waiting for you when you come back."

I nodded. "Thanks."

He nodded in return. "Sure thing. Since you won't be using your house... maybe I could come house sit for you? Turn on the lights and stuff? Chelsea is engaged and the house is turning into a fucking wedding headquarters. It would really help me out to be away from all that frilly shit. I get enough of it at our gigs."

I hadn't even thought of the house but clearly he had. I nodded. "Sure." I hesitated to let James in. I didn't want Stacy to feel awkward around James. I didn't want her to be inconvenienced and there were still things that I wanted to say to her. But now wasn't the right time. I needed to get my head on right and fix myself. Ultimately things needed to be taken care of and James was the guy who was going to be helping. I stepped aside and waited for him to pass before closing the door behind him.

James was standing there in the entryway, his eyes turned towards the direction of my room. He was standing as still as a statue. "What the hell is wrong with you?" As I stepped beside him I realized. Stacy was in my bedroom, her naked body on display through the crack in my door. With a growl and a pinch of jealousy that James' eyes were taking in my woman I pushed him to the side. "Keep it moving."

He fell to the side and moved towards the kitchen, a stupid grin on his face. I moved down the hall and popped my head into my bedroom. "James is here. He saw you naked. If he says anything about it I'll kill him. Sorry." It came out in a rush, she barely had time to comprehend it before I shut the door, closing myself away from her naked body. The temptation was too great.

I made my way towards the kitchen and started up the coffee pot. "I'll let you stay here, but you cannot throw any parties. You cannot fuck anywhere except in the bed." I didn't really like the thought of that either but I knew he was going to do it. I'd buy new sheets once I got out of rehab. Maybe I'd just buy a whole new bed. I stared at the dark brown liquid, the smell of it alone making my mind start churning.

Would Stacy still be single when I got out? Would she want to see me? Would

I be able to make it through rehab and still be someone she wanted? The biggest question of all was how I was going to make it through without seeing her.

"What if she can't control herself and we fuck on the floor?"

"No." The floor was already marked with me and Stacy.

James sighed dramatically. "Alright. The bed only."

"I'll leave my checkbook for when the bills come in." I wondered if James was the right guy for the job. Perhaps someone like Elly would be a better choice. She seemed dependable and responsible. And as far as I knew she wasn't going to be fucking anyone in my house.

"Seriously though, dude, I won't have chicks here. They can't know where I live. They'd never leave me alone."

I shook my head at his logic.

"I was surprised that you took Stacy home when I'd heard about it. But then again, look what happened. She stuck around."

"Yeah, she did." And I considered myself lucky that she had. She deserved better.

James and I both looked up when we heard Stacy clear her throat. "I'd better get going." Her eyes met mine and despite wanting to go over there and kiss her I stayed where I was. I didn't open my arms to her. I nodded. The flash of rejection crossed her beautiful face and I instantly felt like an asshole and regretted it. But it was better this way for now. She looked at James, nodded to him, and then grabbed her things and made for the front door.

It shut behind her quietly. I felt James stare on me as I made myself a cup of coffee.

"Dude. You're gonna regret that."

He didn't have to tell me. I already did.

Stacy

The door clicking shut behind me echoed in my chest. My heart was slamming painfully against my ribs. What had just happened? How did Rio go from sweet post-coital Rio to ass-face Rio so quickly? I felt so stupid for falling for his sweet talk. He loved me? Whatever. I got into my car and then looked at his house one last time. I didn't suspect I'd be back here again anytime soon. Not after that clear dismissal.

On my drive home I replayed my sexy time with Rio in my head. And it had been sexy. And short lived. Just like the last time. I could only hope that this time I wouldn't be pining over him for months: day and night. He was a jerk just like the rest, fully capable of full jerkdom. But what hurt the most was that he'd told me he loved me. And I thought he'd meant it. At least the belief hadn't lasted the course of years. It had only been a few hours.

But thinking he'd meant it had been stupid. We'd known each other all of what? A few months? And he was already declaring his love for me? If I didn't think I had similar feelings for him I'd think it was really creepy.

I spent the rest of the night watching horrible TV and then fell asleep.

The next morning the sun was shining and the birds were singing. My bed was empty and cold everywhere except where my body had warmed it. I was about to get out of bed when my phone rang.

With a groan I picked it up. "Hello?"

"Hey baby. I've missed you. What are you doing?"

I frowned and I wished that there were a button on the phone that would deploy some sort of weapon. Like mace or maybe spider spray. It was Chance. I didn't bother answering him, I hung up immediately.

He called back three more times and each time I let it go to voicemail. I was lacing up my tennis shoes, getting ready for work, when there was a knock on my door. Chance knew where I lived but he'd never come over unannounced, would he?

I bit my lower lip as I stood up and made my way to the door. I peeped through the hole. Rio? I tried to get closer and bumped my head on the door.

"Ow! Damnit." I was rubbing it when I heard his silken voice through the wood.

"You can't hide from me now, Stacy, I know you're in there."

I was still rubbing my forehead when I unlocked and swung the door open. He was standing there, holding out an envelope. I stared at in confusion and he waved it up and down.

"Take it."

I shook my head and tried to appear uninterested. "I'm good."

He sighed, staring me down. "Stacy, come on, just take it."

"What is it?"

"It's a letter. Take it, please."

I was curious now. I grabbed the envelope from him.

He stood there, awkwardly, as he glanced at my outfit. "Are you going to work?"

I glanced down at my uniform and then back to him, unimpressed by his ability to connect the dots. I nodded.

"Well, just... save that for after work then. Sorry, I didn't realize." He held up his hand and then turned away, heading down the hallway where he'd come from. I was going to call out to him but his long legs carried him too quickly away. I stared at the white envelope in my hand. I was itching to open it. But there must have been a reason why he didn't want me to open it right away so I left it on my side table by the door. I'd put my stuff on it later and then I would remember.

Little did I know I didn't need to put it somewhere I'd remember it because it was all I could think about the entire time I was on shift. By the time I came home

I was practically tearing the thing open. Little bits of paper floated to the floor in my fervor. Was he apologizing for the way he'd left things? For the things he didn't say? For acting like we were strangers in his kitchen with James right in front of us?

I was panting softly as I unfolded the letter and began to read.

Stacy,

I wanted to let you know that I'm checking myself into rehab tonight. I wanted to tell you that I'm sorry for the way things went down between us. I hope that I haven't hurt you in any way. I regret sleeping with you the second time. I shouldn't have said those words. First rule in AA is that you need to take things slow. Now that I've fallen off the wagon it's going to mean my starting over. And that means that whatever was between us, whatever I said, it doesn't matter anymore. I hope you understand.

Rio

I felt tears prick my eyes as I re-read the letter once again, taking my time, letting his words soak in. He regretted it. He regretted it all. I was such a fool to think otherwise. Such a fool to hope that he had feelings for me beyond the physical attraction. I folded up the letter carefully and put it into the drawer of the side table. The next time I had feelings for him, or thoughts about us together, I'd pull out that letter and read it again.

Whatever hopes I'd had of not feeling anything for Rio were crushed. He was in my heart. He'd replaced Chance the instant he'd smiled at me on Christmas Eve after we'd wiped the floor with Elly and Kent at the pool table. Love at first sight wasn't supposed to be a thing. But it felt like it had been for me.

I was such a fool.

Chapter 23

Rio

I arrived at the cemetery an hour before the sun was due to set. I only had an hour to talk to my sister and then I needed to check myself into rehab. I parked on the road and walked the rest of the way to her grave. I wiped the dirt from her headstone and then sat down on the grass. I stared at her name for a long minute. In my head I remembered what she'd looked like and her smile. My baby sister was always so full of life when my mother had been alive before the car accident that had taken her life.

"Hey." I looked around, the birds were getting noisy in the trees as they settled in for the evening. I looked back to her headstone. "So, I've been seeing this girl, Stacy. Well, not really seeing her. I haven't taken her on dates, not really. There's just something about her. She just breathes life. When I'm around her she just... She brings me back to life. And she's so beautiful." I looked down at my hands, full of grass I'd plucked. "I told her I loved her. And I meant it. And that's the scariest shit I've faced since... well, since I thought she might be dying. But before that, it was you. Losing you." I wiped my hands roughly on my jeans, gathering the strength to say the words. "I wish I could have saved you from him. It will always be a regret I have. I will always carry blame for what happened to you." I clenched my jaw and swallowed back the pain. "But I'm trying to be the kind of guy you'd be proud to call your big brother. I'm trying to be everything he wasn't. But some days I feel like I'm failing and I look in the mirror and I see him. Whenever I was drinking, I saw him in myself and it scared the shit out of me. I can't be that guy - the guy who goes on a bender and just disregards everyone else's feelings. I can't go down the slippery slope because someday I'll find myself hitting someone I love, just like our father. And I'll lose everything in the process. I want to be the guy worthy of being with Stacy. I'm not sure if I believe in God or not but when I think to myself in rehab I'll be sending my thoughts to you. If there is a God I know he would've put you up there in heaven with him."

I heard leaves crunching behind me and when I turned around I saw a man coming up towards me. I stood quickly and wiped the dirt from my pants. My eyes hardened the closer he got. His face was, unfortunately, forever ingrained into my mind and my DNA.

"Son. I didn't expect to see you here."

"Likewise. But I was just leaving." I made a move to go but he held up his hand to stop me.

"Wait. There's something I wanted to tell you."

"There's nothing I need to hear from you." I started walking away. I was a grown man who was about to go to rehab so I could try to remove all traces of my self-blame that my father had caused. I didn't need him stirring up even more shit for me.

"Johnny, please."

I stopped cold when he spoke my name. The name I shared with him. The name I'd gotten rid of the instant I left home. While I was reeling from the memories of everything associated with that name he started to talk.

"I'm sorry for the kind of man I became after your mom died. I wasn't a father to you, I was... I was a fucked up grieving man. You have no idea how much I regret that I didn't get help or take help when it was there for me. I regret so much but mostly I regret what I did to you kids. There is no excuse and I don't blame you for staying away and shutting me out. I died along with your mama. But I shouldn't have. I should've stayed alive for you and your sister. I'm sorry."

I took his apology and I pocketed it. I unclenched the fists I didn't know I'd clenched and continued to walk towards my bike. His apology was nothing, because as he'd said, he was already dead to me. It was his fault I was an alcoholic. It was his fault that my sister had died.

I stopped when I was nearly to my bike and looked over my shoulder. My father was standing by Penny's grave, his head hung down with his hands in his pockets. I stalked back. There was something I wanted to say to him. Something I'd been dying to say to him for years. And now was the time to let it out. He was here in the flesh and he was sober, as far as I could tell.

"Fuck you!"

He looked up, surprise coloring his thin face. He opened his mouth to say something but I spoke first.

"Fuck you for ruining my fucking chance at having something good! Fuck you for ruining her life because you're a narcissistic asshole! Fuck you for teaching me that the way to deal with grief is through drowning myself in a fucking bottle!" My fists were clenched at my sides, my body was tight with unsprung tension. I wanted to hit him. I wanted to hit him for all the times he hit me and my sister. But then I wouldn't be any better than he was. "Fuck you for being a shitty fucking father when we needed you the most."

As I drove away and headed toward rehab I felt liberated and drained all at the same time. I wanted her. I wanted Stacy. I wanted to tell her everything that had just happened. But she wasn't my girlfriend. She wasn't my wife. She wasn't anything but a past relationship that I had royally fucked up. The baggage I'd carried around for years had been holding me back from life. I wasn't going to let it anymore. As long as it took I'd be in rehab. And when I finally got out I was going to go back for Stacy. She was the one I wanted to go forward in life with. I only hoped she felt the same when she saw the new me.

Stacy

Graduation day was upon me! I was all smiles as I turned my tassel to the other side and accepted my rolled up piece of paper that signified the diploma I'd later receive in the mail. I couldn't believe this day had finally come! There was something to be said for being single and against dating. I ended my school year with a bang. I had lots of money saved up from working and not spending it on manicures or clothes or makeup AND I had gotten all A's in every single course.

It was getting to the point where I was okay being Stacy. Just Stacy. Not Stacy, the girlfriend of whatever jerk my libido thought was hot.

As people ushered out of the stadium and went to greet their families I rushed towards the other row of seats where Elly was. We hugged and bounced up and down.

"Oh my god! We did it!"

"We did!" I glanced around briefly, searching for any familiar faces. "Your mom is here?"

Elly nodded. "Yeah! She's making me lunch so we won't have to be jam packed in with everyone else trying to get a table at the Olive Garden. Do you want to come?"

"Oh. I mean, I would but I have a date at my place with my mom and pizza delivery."

"I still can't believe you're leaving us and going to Chicago!"

I couldn't help but grin. I'd gotten myself the best internship opportunity that had been available to me and I was leaving to fulfill my destiny in four short days. "I know. But I'll be back before you know it." I looked around for my mother when my eyes fell on Rio. I gasped softly. He was dressed up in a black button down shirt, red tie and black slacks. And he'd cut his hair.

My eyes left him and went to James and Frank as they all approached the two of us. They were all here. For Elly. I smiled politely and listened as they all congratulated her and gave her hugs. How nice that Elly had another mini-family. I pressed my lips together and looked away, I didn't want to ruin my mascara or cry in front of the guys. Working and doing school work had been great but it had been lonely.

It wasn't until Elly's mom came over that I looked up again, hoping she'd drawn all the attention away. My eyes were drawn to him and his eyes were already on me. His hands were stuffed in his pockets as he took a step closer, blocking my view of everyone else.

"Congratulations, Stacy."

I nodded and smiled politely, hiding what was really churning inside me with everything that I had. "Thanks."

He nodded back. I felt his eyes taking me in. There wasn't much to take in. I was covered with a big black gown.

"How are you?" When I looked up his eyes were still staring at me. Why was he trying so hard to make small talk with me?

"I'm good." I turned to Elly and grabbed onto her sleeve. "Hey, I'll stop by before I go, okay? I'm going to go say hi to a few people."

Elly turned to me and smiled. "Okay." She gave me one more hug and then pulled away, posing with her mom while James snapped a few pictures. Rio was still watching me. I smiled politely at him and then gave him a little wave.

I stared like a dummy for a few seconds waiting for him to return it. But he didn't. I turned away and started walking towards my car. There wasn't anyone else I wanted to say hi to. I'd lied about that part. I pulled my hat off and stared at it. It meant so much. I smiled and tucked it under my arm as I ran a hand through my hair, fluffing it up a little.

I was halfway there when I heard someone jogging behind me. My heart was flip-flopping in my chest. Stupid heart. Didn't it know that Rio was not interested? "Forget something?" I asked, still walking.

"I just wanted to make sure you got to your car okay."

I chuckled, "I'm a big girl with a college degree. I think I can manage getting to my car okay."

He was silent for a few moments as he walked beside me, his hands stuffed in his pockets. "Then you're going to make me admit that I wanted to see you for a few more minutes."

My gut fluttered and my heart flip-flopped again.

"I don't know why you'd want to do that." I tried to play it off and act all cool. Inside I was losing it. I hated that he had that effect on me. Soon it wouldn't matter and I'd be safely away from him in Chicago. "You made it pretty clear a few months ago that we had a good time but that was over. And I'm over it. Aren't you?" I dared a glance at him. He was staring at the ground as we walked. I pulled my gaze away from him and refocused on my car. I didn't know what game he was playing but I wasn't interested. We were finally at my car. I unlocked it and threw my stuff into the backseat. "Look, I don't want to play games with you. I'm moving away in a few days and I'm not really looking for another roll around your bed."

He had stopped on the curb and stuffed his hands into his pockets. His jaw twitched and he looked away towards the horizon. "So you've already taken a job?"

"Yeah. I took it a few weeks ago. And I found a nice apartment and I'm thinking about getting a dog."

He nodded, his jaw still twitching under his cheek as his familiar blue eyes settled on my face. There was an awkward pause and then all at once he freed his hands and wrapped his arms around me. I closed my eyes tightly together. Didn't he know that his closeness, his touch, would undo me? I weakly hugged him back, defeated. When he moved I was sure he was going to pull away, put his macho stand-offish stance back on, but he surprised me again by pressing his lips to mine.

He tested my reaction first, his lips on mine gently and then he pressed forward, pressed them more firmly to mine as his hand pressed into my backside to make sure our bodies were as close as they could be.

He was so cruel. So very cruel. I pulled my face away and tried to put my hands between us to push him off.

"I've gotta go."

To my relief and disappointment he let me go and stayed on the curb as I pulled my car out of its spot and drove away. I watched his form get smaller and smaller in the rearview. It was for the best.

Chapter 24

7 months later...

Rio

It was killing me to wait here like this knowing that Stacy was in the same building but that I couldn't see her right away. I had managed to get it out of Elly that Stacy was going to be back for Christmas. I'd managed to get a lot of things out of Elly in regards to Stacy's well-being over the past seven months. She'd been doing really well in Chicago but she hated the big city life. It felt unfair that I knew all of these things about Stacy but I couldn't keep myself from asking the questions.

I crossed my arms and tried to stay still as I stared at the group of people flowing into the baggage claim area. None of the faces were familiar. I stared at the time and shook my head. This was definitely her flight. Slowly the amount of people coming in trickled off. Still no sign of Stacy. I gave it five more minutes before pushing off the wall and heading for the nearest information center.

"Excuse me, flight 2495 has landed, right?"

"Yes, sir," the woman, in her late fifties smiled politely. It probably sucked for her having to work Christmas Eve.

"Can you tell me if someone was on that flight?"

"No, sir, I'm sorry. Sometimes passengers get held up or stop inside the terminal for food."

I nodded, not really liking her lack of answers but I wasn't about to yell at her for it. She was just doing her job. I pushed off the desk and ran smack into someone. "Oh, dammit, I'm sorry!" I grabbed onto the person and had every intention of helping to steady them but when I looked down my eyes met with Stacy's. My heart seized in my chest and I held onto her.

"Rio?" She looked every bit as surprised as I did. But of course she would, she had no idea I was coming. She glanced to the man I hadn't noticed standing beside her and stepped back from me. I took inventory of the man, sizing him up. He was slightly shorter than me, with light colored hair that was probably sporting one of those hundred dollar haircuts. He was dressed like he was from the city too in a pair of dark slacks, shiny black shoes, and a green sweater. His eyes were doing the same assessment of me. I clenched my jaw tightly. Elly hadn't mentioned some other man. Maybe Elly didn't know. Maybe it was meant to be a surprise.

"Rio, this is Thomas. He was my in-flight companion." She smiled, her cheeks flushed with pink. Was she blushing because of me or this dude?

I held out my hand and Thomas shook it. "Nice to meet you, Rio." He dropped my hand and looked down to Stacy. There was hope in his eyes. "So maybe I'll catch you on the flight back?"

She returned the smile and pushed some of her hair behind her ear, nodding. "Yeah. Maybe so. Merry Christmas," she said.

"Merry Christmas."

They waved awkwardly and then he was gone. Stacy looked around the baggage claim before meeting my gaze again. "What are you doing here? Are you expecting someone?"

I nodded. "You."

Her smile dropped. "Did something happen to Elly? Is she alright?"

"She's fine. I offered to take over the job so she could spend the time with her family."

She looked me over and nodded. "Must be a hard time of the year for you," she said softly, her eyes looking over my face. My lips itched to kiss hers.

I cleared my throat to get those thoughts out of my head. "It is what it is. Let's get your bag and then I'll take you to your mom's."

The first half of the car trip was quiet, only the sound of Anaheim Steamroller moved through the van. I tried getting her to open up a little but nothing seemed to work.

"How are you?" she asked, her eyes on the road when I snuck a glance.

"Not good."

She twisted in her seat, worry on her face. "You're not good? Have you been going to your meetings? Did something happen?"

I cleared my throat. "I fucked up this thing with this woman."

"Oh." She started to turn around in her seat but my hand on her knee stopped her.

"It was seven months ago but it still hurts. A lot." I let that sink in a moment before I continued. "I told this woman that I loved her and then I pushed her away because I was going through some stuff. I didn't think I was worthy of her so I had to let her go. Not for me but for her."

"Rio, stop the car."

I felt the slam of panic in my chest as I pulled the van over to the side of the road. As soon as I clicked the gear shift into park I turned to look at her. Her face was unreadable, like she was wearing a mask.

"What are you doing?" she asked, her body tense and uncomfortable looking. How could I blame her? The last time I'd seen her I'd kissed her even though I hadn't been ready. I'd been aching for the past seven months to do it again. This time I was ready. I was going regularly to talk to someone about the ghosts of my past. I just needed to show Stacy that I was finally ready to be the man she needed. At least I hope I could be that for her.

"I'm trying to apologize, maybe?"

"Apologize for what? You don't have anything to say you're sorry for." Her green eyes, dark in the dim light of my van, searched my face.

A small chuckle left my chest. "I have so much to apologize for." She stared at me, as if waiting for my confession. I wasn't ready to let it all out just yet. She'd just push me away. I saw it already in her body which was coiled tightly. She was already resisting me. "But don't worry. I'm not going to throw it all at you right now. I'm not going to convince you to jump into bed with me. I'm not going anywhere fast, Stacy. I'm going to be here."

She licked her lips slowly and then nibbled on the lower one as she turned back around in her seat. "And I'm not," she said softly. It was so soft I wasn't sure I'd heard her right. "I'm staying in Chicago."

Stacy

The rest of the trip to my mama's house had been silent and awkward. I hadn't thought it was going to be so hard to break the news to Rio. And if I thought telling Rio had been hard I couldn't imagine what it was going to feel like once I told my mama. After everything I'd said to her about moving home to be close to her I had decided against it.

I planned to pay her back, every cent, for what she'd put towards my college expenses. My boss had offered me benefits and a very nice salary in exchange for full time employment in Chicago. I'd have been a fool to turn it down. It was very generous and a good career move. And when I'd written out my pros and cons list the only bad thing had been mama. I figured I could convince her to move up to Chicago with me. It was cold up there but there was lots of culture.

Rio stopped the van in the dirt driveway and turned off the engine. We both sat there for a long moment. I was waiting for him to say something. Maybe he was waiting for me to say something.

"Thanks for the ride, Rio. I'll get my bag and get out of your hair." I hopped out of the car, the deflated feeling in my chest was a little too familiar whenever I was around Rio. I had expected him to grab me and pull me close to him and kiss me until I conceded to doing whatever it was he wanted to do. I was surprised when I'd come around the back of the van and saw him pulling my suitcase out. I smiled softly as I reached out to take it from him. He grunted and jerked it slightly out of my grasp.

"I've got it. Not going to let you carry your bag."

I nodded my thanks and led the way towards my mama's trailer door. His footsteps were loud and sure behind me. We stopped on the doormat and faced each other. I blew out a little breath. "So..."

He nodded and dropped his gaze. "Yeah."

Before I could make an excuse not to I wrapped my arms around his shoulders and pulled my body in close to him. I inhaled slowly, trying to memorize his scent. I'd missed him more than I had a right to. "Merry Christmas," I whispered as his arm moved around me and held me to his body. He seemed to be breathing me in at the same rate that I was. I closed my eyes tightly and for a moment I let myself imagine that it was something I didn't have to try to commit to memory.

I mustered up enough strength to pull myself away and managed one more quick smile.

"Merry Christmas," he said as his eyes took in my face.

I looked towards the door handle. I had to look everywhere but at him. If I stared at him staring at me with those wistful eyes I was going to do something really stupid. I cleared my throat and knocked on the door. The twinkling of the white Christmas lights illuminated the porch surprisingly well.

I reached for the suitcase once more and he reluctantly let it go. "I think I can manage from here," I said and nodded towards his car, giving him the signal that it was time for him to go.

"Alright," he said. He stuffed his hands into the pockets of his jeans and then stared at me for another long moment. He nodded and reluctantly left me standing there on my mama's porch. I huffed out a breath I hadn't known I'd been holding and turned to face the door fully. He was in the past. I had to let him stay there.

I knocked on the door again. "Mama, it's me! Open up!" I took a couple of steps to the side and tried to see past the curtains that were hanging on the window. There was only a small sliver of room for me to peek in and I couldn't see anything but Christmas tree.

I sighed and glanced back over my shoulder. Rio was still sitting in the driveway, his eyes on me. I had just spoken to my mama before I hopped on the plane. She knew I was coming. I knocked once more and tried the handle. Luckily it was unlocked.

I pushed my way inside and glanced around. The TV was on but the couch was empty. The artificial tree smell that my mom loved filled the trailer. I put my suitcase down and tried to shake off the feeling that something wasn't right.

"Mama?" I closed the front door behind me and moved into the tiny kitchen. The Christmas tree candle was sitting on the counter, the flame barely visible at the bottom of the jar. I reached out to blow it out and instantly yelped the instant my hand met with the hot glass. That candle had been burning for hours. That wasn't like mama. The hairs on the back of my neck raised as I quickly walked through the rest of the trailer, steeling myself for whatever I was about to find. Something definitely wasn't right.

"Mama?" I called out again just before turning the corner to my mama's room. She was laying on her bed, her eyes on the ceiling. When she heard me her eyes moved to me. Relief washed over me as I moved to the side of the bed. "Mama, Jesus! I thought you were dead."

With eyes on me she started mumbling nonsense. I frowned and put my hand on her head. She didn't feel feverish. "Mama? Are you okay?"

She blinked three times in a row and I felt my heart sink again. Whenever I was crying so hard as a child that I couldn't speak my mama and I would use a blinking signal. One blink was yes. Three blinks was no. Quickly I ran back into the living room and retrieved my cellphone from my purse. I dialed 9-1-1 and ran back into my mama's room.

"Hello, 9-1-1, what is your emergency?"

Chapter 25

Rio

I don't know why I'd decided to stay. Maybe I was hoping I'd get to see her through the kitchen window. But I'd stayed. When I saw Stacy running through the kitchen and then back again I had the feeling something wasn't right. I got out of my van and went to the front door, knocking loudly. I counted to thirty before trying the handle.

Once inside I heard Stacy's weak panicked voice. "Yes, she's talking but I can't understand her. She's just laying here. I–"

I quickly found her in her mother's bedroom. She didn't see me or she refused to acknowledge my presence. I stood up behind her and waited for the phone call to end. My heart was pounding in my chest and my heart was hurting for her to see her mother like this. I sent a thousand silent prayers up to heaven, praying that her mama would be okay. I knew the pain and anguish losing a parent would cause. I didn't want that for Stacy. Not for a long, long time.

She must have finally felt my warmth behind her because she turned around. When she tilted her head back and looked at me I saw the unshed tears in her eyes. She was barely holding herself together. But she was doing it. I opened my arm, offering her my solace. Silently she stepped beside me and leaned on me. I closed my eyes tightly as I held her protectively against me. If I'd have left her she would've been dealing with this all alone on Christmas Eve.

The paramedics arrived shortly after the phone call had ended. I stood nearby as Stacy talked to her mom and held onto her hand and assured her that everything was going to be okay. I stood beside Stacy as they took her mouth out of the trailer on the gurney. All the neighbors were outside their trailers staring at the drama that was unfolding in the trailer park. A few of them came by to ask Stacy if she needed anything. Stacy declined. Once they double tapped on the door they pulled away, taking Stacy's mom to the hospital. Their initial diagnosis was that her mom was most likely having a stroke. The sirens went on and the lights quickly disappeared.

As more folks approached I wrapped my arm around Stacy and ushered her back into the trailer. She glanced behind us towards my van. "Not yet, Stacy. They're going to take care of her and we'll go see her soon. You don't want to be there in all the rush. You'll just be pacing around waiting to hear something. They know who she is, they know you're coming to be with her."

"But what if..."

"No," I stopped her train wreck of a thought. "She's going to be okay. That was not goodbye forever."

"You can't know that!" Her tears were finally escaping in the privacy of her mama's trailer. I moved over the kitchen window and pulled the curtains shut. We needed privacy. She needed privacy.

"I do. In my gut, I know it." It was a lie, I didn't know it. But it wasn't going to do her any good to be in the hospital waiting and worrying over something she couldn't control. I grabbed a couple of mugs from the cupboard and put them on the counter. "Do you want coffee first or a shower first?" I glanced behind me at the silence that responded. Stacy wasn't there. I looked around quickly and saw her dashing out the front door.

"Goddamnit!" I raced after her and barely made it in time to open the passenger door and jump in. She was in the driver's seat, her hands shaking, tears streaking down her cheeks.

"I'm sorry, Rio but I have to be there!"

I held onto the dashboard as she hit the gas and then the brake, whipping us both forward. With a grunt I reached over and buckled her into her seat and then I did the same for me.

"Just... don't get us killed, Stacy. I'm not ready to die yet."

She sniffled and eased up on the gas a little.

I couldn't look at the road so I took the opportunity to stare at Stacy. It had been seven long months but she hadn't changed. She was still as beautiful as ever. Her auburn hair curved against her shoulders and her lips were full and shining. Her cheeks were slightly rounded, her chin came to a tasteful point. Her neck was probably one of my favorite features. She held her head up high, no slouching and it left lots of bare skin between her ear and her shoulder. I closed my eyes and looked away. I shouldn't be lusting after her when she was in a state of panic.

With a slow reach I placed my hand on Stacy's leg. She jumped but quickly eased into the feeling of my hand on her.

"Thank you for being there," she said softly, her voice a quiver.

"Stacy, there isn't anywhere else I'd be. I'll be there for you as much as you'll let me." We sat in silence with those words between us for a moment before her hand left the steering wheel and joined mine.

After parking and checking in with the nurses, we went to the waiting room and sat down. I sat down. She paced. I crossed my arms over my chest after shooting a text message to Elly. I exhaled slowly and watched her. She paced back and forth across the space unless a nurse or doctor started walking towards the waiting area. She resumed her pacing every time they didn't stop in to talk to her.

I was just about to grab her and hold her down on my lap when a doctor came over. "Ms. Hammond?" His eyes latched onto Stacy and he nodded as he came to stand in front of her. I moved to stand behind her, putting my hand on her shoulder as a show of support. Her hand covered mine as she waited for the news. "Ms. Hammond, your mother had a stroke." He assessed Stacy's composure before continuing. "She's lucky she arrived when she did but unfortunately some damage had already been done."

I felt her body catch itself. I came closer and put my other hand at her hip.

"She's probably not going to be the woman she was before the stroke, but it's likely she'll regain most of her speech and movements back with rehabilitation and time."

Stacy was nodding, I could feel her body quivering under my hands.

"We are going to keep her here for a few nights to make sure that she doesn't undergo another stroke. So for now there isn't much you can do except wait, unfortunately. We're going to take good care of her." He cleared his throat as he pulled out a little booklet and handed it to her. "Go see her for yourself and then head home and read through this. There's lots of important information in there and it will prepare you for what's ahead."

She took the pamphlet and stared at it for a long moment. More nodding.

"What room is she in?" I asked.

"812."

"Thank you," I said and nodded, letting him know he could go about his duties. I waited until he was gone to step beside Stacy. With my hand on her back I guided her towards her mother's room. "Come on, Stacy. You ready?"

She wouldn't budge. When I turned to look at her those teary eyes were back. I pulled her into my chest and covered her body with my arms as she cried into my chest.

"Worst. Christmas. Ever," she cried.

Stacy

We walked into my mama's trailer just before midnight. "Do you want something to drink or eat?" I asked. I didn't feel like being hospitable but it was Rio and he'd been there for me tonight when I'd needed him.

"No, Stacy. I'm fine. Do you want me to stay here tonight?" I heard his boots clunking on the floor as he stepped up behind me. I could feel his warmth but I didn't turn around to look at him. I couldn't. I didn't have any energy left.

I did want him to stay but I didn't want to ruin his Christmas. But then again he had no family. It was probably the least I could do to let him stay if he wanted to stay. I turned around and leaned back against the counter. He looked so strong and capable like he could go at least three more rounds.

"If you don't have anywhere else you need to be. I don't want to take away from your plans."

He stepped forward and covered my arms with his large hands. Slowly they moved up and down, warming me. "No plans." He pressed a kiss to my head and then stepped back. Almost instantly I missed his warmth. "I'll take the couch."

"You can sleep in my bed and I'll sleep in my mama's bed. Follow me and I'll get you settled." I led the way to my tiny bedroom still decorated with posters and magazine cutouts from my youth.

He grinned as he surveyed my room. I rolled my eyes and shoved him inside. His large frame made the room seem so small. "Shut up and go to bed."

"Yes, ma'am." The grin was still plastered all over his face.

I rolled my eyes and went across the hall. My suitcase was in there already. Rio must have moved it amid all the chaos of earlier. It was all I could do to move to the bed. My body was drained of everything. Sleep couldn't come fast enough.

In the morning I woke up to the sound of Frank Sinatra crooning in the kitchen. The sweet smell of something baking wafted throughout the trailer. Still dressed in last night's clothes, I decided to go ahead and take a shower before venturing out into the kitchen. Once I was cleaning I made my way towards the commotion and the good smells.

Rio heard me coming. He was at the stove, my mother's pink "Caution: I can go from hostess to bitch in 2.5 seconds" apron around his body. "Merry Christmas," he said, an enthusiastic smile on his face.

"You're in an awful good mood."

"Of course I am. I'm with you."

I tried not to let his words affect me but they went right to my cheeks, heating them and turning shades of pink. My eyes drifted away and I searched for anything other than his eyes to look at.

"Are those supposed to be Santa Claus heads?"

He glanced down at the finished pancake sitting on the plate and scowled. "No, they're Christmas trees." He held the plate up for a closer inspection.

I shook my head as I walked towards him and gave him a pity pat on his back. "You need to practice a bit more."

"I hope you're hungry anyway. These fucked up Christmas pancakes aren't going to eat themselves."

"I am, actually. They smell delicious."

"Good. Have a seat and I'll serve you."

I took a seat at the table and couldn't help but show a little grin. "A girl could get used to this."

He put the pancakes in the middle of the table along with syrup and butter, poured us both coffee, and then joined me at the table. "Good. My plan is working."

I knew he was teasing but the blush came back all the same. We ate and chatted about what had been going on in our lives since graduation. It was so good catching up with him. He always made me feel so comfortable. We laughed and by the end of the meal I had completely forgotten that this had been the worst Christmas of my life.

We cleaned the dishes together and that's when things grew serious again.

"What are you going to do about Chicago?" he asked, handing me a dripping plate.

I wiped the water off before putting it away, giving myself some time to muster up a response. The truth was I hadn't even thought about Chicago. I hadn't fully wrapped my head around what this would mean. A few months ago mama's relationship with Hank had ended. Obviously there was no new man in the picture. She only had me.

"I'm going to have to turn down the job, I guess." Admittedly I was sad. And partially relieved. Maybe this was God intervening in my life. A fucked up way to go about it but he had gotten his point across. I wasn't going to be staying in Chicago. My mama needed me here.

"I'm sorry," he said, handing me another plate. "I know you were looking forward to that job. The money."

"Mama is more important," I said with finality. "I bet you're relieved."

He handed me the next dish, one eyebrow cocked. "Oh?"

"Now you can start apologizing for the past. And try to make it up to me. Because now I'm not going anywhere either."

"I feel like an asshole," he said, his hands pressed against the edge of the sink, his whole body hunched over as if in anguish.

"Why do you feel like an asshole?"

"Because I'm so happy that you're staying here."

My heart skipped a beat as I stared at him. Slowly his face turned towards mine and his eyes moved over my face. I moved towards him, like a moth to a flame, only slower. He turned his body towards me too and moved a hand into my hair. He cupped my neck and pulled me towards him. His lips pressed to mine. He wanted to go slow, I could feel the hesitation but it had been seven months since I'd last kissed him. And I'd missed him. I grabbed onto him and pulled him back with me. Our kisses were feverish and hot. He grabbed onto me and placed me on top of the counter. My legs went around his waist, pulling him closer.

With a groan he pulled back. "Stacy. God how I've missed you."

"Then shut up and kiss me."

He groaned again, sounding in pain. "Only if you promise that this isn't some distraction for you. To try to take your mind off your mama."

"It's not." I grabbed onto the back of his neck and pulled his lips to mine. Rio was safety and comfort and home. He was everything I'd been missing and denying myself. And here he was throwing himself at me. I wasn't going to waste it.

We lay in the middle of my tiny twin bed, one on top of the other after a hot round of sex. I had my ear to his chest listening intently as his heart thumped. I thought maybe I was dreaming. It wouldn't be the first time I had thought about Rio. About this with Rio. I inhaled deeply, closing my eyes, breathing him in. I didn't ever want to forget it.

His fingers were stroking along my naked back lazily, pulling me from my thoughts.

"Merry Christmas," I said as I lifted my head and met his eyes.

He lifted the corners of his mouth in a lazy grin. "Merry Christmas, indeed."

I moved up his body slowly and pressed my lips to his. The innocent kisses soon turned into heated ones. Just as I moved my hand down his body there was a loud knocking at the front door.

"Stacy! Rio! Let us in!"

We both groaned as soon as we recognized Elly's voice.

"Damnit. I texted her this morning to let her know we'd be here."

I pinched his nipple and forced myself to get up. "Way to kill the mood."

"I'm sorry," he said as he rolled off my tiny bed which squeaked from the bulk of him.

"Bah-humbug."

We both dressed quickly and answered the door. Elly was there along with James and Frank.

"Hey, Stacy!" Elly came forward and wrapped me up in a hug. She pulled back after a minute and looked me over. I heard the other two head towards the kitchen with Rio. "I'm so sorry about your mom. Is she going to be alright?" There was genuine concern in her eyes and it still moved me that I had a friend as caring as she was.

I nodded a little. "The doctor said she might get much better. With time and therapy."

"Are you going to hire someone to take care of her?"

"I mean, I think I'll have to while I'm at work. But I'll be here in the evenings and on weekends."

Elly frowned slightly. "So you're staying here? What about Chicago?"

I shrugged my shoulders and peeked over my shoulder at Rio who was feeding the rest of his Christmas rejected pancakes to the guys. "I'm not going back, Elly." My voice dropped to a whisper. "I wasn't really happy there anyway."

"Do you need a job? Do you have anything saved up? Can I help at all?"

I smiled softly and shook my head. "That's very sweet of you, Elly. But I'll figure it out." I hugged her again and we joined the guys in the kitchen. For the next few hours we ate and laughed and sang Christmas carols. It was almost as if life were normal. Almost.

Chapter 26

Rio

"So, did you and Stacy kiss and make up yet?" James asked as we stepped outside. Elly and the gang had been here for a few hours and I could see it was wearing on Stacy.

"That's not really any of your business."

He grinned and smacked me hard on the back. I grunted and clenched my jaw so I wouldn't do something equally juvenile, like whack him in the nut sack. "You dog. So she finally tamed the Rio-beast?"

"More like she finally let the Rio-beast sleep on the floor." James had come to visit me every Saturday and we waxed intellectual on a few levels. I knew about his past with Teagan, the girl who broke his heart. And he finally knew about my feelings for Stacy.

He clapped me on the shoulder again before opening his car door. "You're still closer than I am to finding the lady I'm going to stick it to for the rest of my life."

"Can't imagine why," I replied dryly. "Thanks for coming over. I don't know if it helped but it definitely distracted her for a little while."

James nodded, "Just say 'free food' and I'll come running." He grinned and ducked into his car. As he started it Frank and Elly came out.

I opened the door for Elly, giving her a hug before she crawled into the backseat.

"Take it easy, man," Frank said.

I nodded and shut the door behind them. I watched as they pulled out into the street and let out a heavy sigh when they finally disappeared. It was me and Stacy again.

I found myself sitting at the foot of Stacy's bed, her feet in my lap.

"That was exhausting. Is it terrible that I was ready for them to leave a couple of hours ago?" she asked, her arm draped over her eyes.

"No," I said softly, taking one of her feet in my hands. I slowly because to stroke the bottom, testing her to see if she liked it. A soft moan escaped from her throat so I continued. "Do you want to go see your mom?"

"I called the hospital. She's still mostly resting. They assured me that she would be fine without a visitor tonight. I'm still overly tired and overwhelmed." She wiggled her toes and stretched her foot. "That feels really good."

I smiled to myself. "Do you want me to cook you something?"

"No. Just keep doing more of that." She pulled her foot away and held the other up for me to work on. "Rio..." she said, dropping her arm to the bed, unveiling her eyes. "Did you mean what you said on the way here? Do you really want to give us another go?"

I met her eyes and nodded. "I do. I want to do it right this time. I want to be a man you'll be proud to stand beside at a Me First and the Gimmie Gimmies concert. I want you to introduce me to everyone as your man."

She smiled at me softly. "A girl could get used to that. But why should I give you another chance?"

"Because what I said, that night, what I said when my mouth was uninhibited. It was true. I was going to wait a year, that was the plan. And if you weren't back by then I was going to fly up there to Chicago and find you and woo you."

"Stalk me?" She grinned, teasing me, but it didn't feel like a joke.

"Beg you." I gently set her feet down in my lap again. "I've missed you so damn much." The silence drug on between us for what seemed like hours before she finally spoke.

She sat up and moved her body until she was sitting in my lap, our arms went around each other and she whispered against my lips. "I missed you too. Maybe this was a blessing in deep disguise."

The thought alone had my heart hammering in my chest. As much as I'd hated to be vulnerable and think that a woman other than my sister and mother had finally mattered in my life, I hated thinking even more that there would never be someone I'd love. And I'd found that love with Stacy. I couldn't explain it and I'd tried many times to explain it to James. She had made me feel whole. She had broken past my shield and forced her way into my life. She'd woken the parts of me that were dead. Since she'd been gone in Chicago those parts had faded again. I wasn't interested in other women. I wasn't interested in much at all except finding ways to change the topic of conversation back to Stacy whenever I had Elly alone.

"Maybe," I said, my voice thick and strange to my own ears. She kept her arms around my neck and I found my hand tangled up in her hair. I'd meant to move it back from her face but I didn't want to let her go.

"I'm willing to give us a try, Rio." Her words were music to my ears but my smile faltered when hers didn't come. She had a stern expression on her face. "But..."

I groaned softly. Buts were never good. "But?"

"But I can't leave my mama. Not until she's recovered. And there's a chance that might never happen. I don't want to hold you back in life. I don't want..." She dropped her gaze to my chest before going on. "I don't want you to give up on marriage and babies and things like that because you're waiting around for me."

I shook my head. "Don't kill us off right from the start. You want to be exclusive, I'm yours."

She looked up, her green eyes sparkling with unshed tears. "Really?"

"I've been yours, Stacy. Since the day we met. Should we just go ahead and get married?"

Her eyes widened with surprise. "Married?" She shook her head. "No. No I don't think I ever want to get married. Is that a deal breaker for you?"

For now? No, it wasn't a deal breaker. In the future? Maybe, but I couldn't live there. I needed to live in the present.

"Come here," I murmured, pulling her closer. She sighed heavily as she wrapped her arms around me and pulled herself against my body, her cheek resting on my shoulder. "Everything will work out, Stacy." I pressed a soft kiss to her hair as I settled her in my arms. "You'll see."

Chapter 27

TEN YEARS AND THREE MONTHS LATER...

Stacy

"Rio! I'm here, are you ready to go?" I stepped into his house, my keys jingling with my every step. It had been a long day at the small accounting firm I'd been working at for the past eight years, and I had huge news to share about mama and Hugh, mama's old physical therapist. They were moving in together and I couldn't be happier for them both. Finally mama had found a man who was worthy of her. Someone who treated her with respect, had a job, and had no intention of ever leaving it. She was leaving the trailer park and that finally meant I could leave it too.

Mama had worked hard to regain everything that she'd lost after the stroke but the left side of her face still sagged, never having fully recovered. She was still just as beautiful in my eyes and happily, she was beautiful in Hugh's eyes too. Rio and I had discussed and argued many times about my living with mama. I was adamant that I was going to stick around to make sure she didn't fall back into her old pattern of doing things. Early on she was focused on recovery but once she was mostly recovered she had reverted back to her old ways of doing things. New men would drive her home from her job at the diner. I made sure I gave each one of them the stink eye and on more than one occasion I had to interrupt bedroom activities. She was mad as a snake at me while it was happening but eventually she forgave me.

I glanced at my phone, noting the time. It was late; later than I'd intended to get here. But still, he should've been here. He'd finished his engineering degree and decided to open up his own engineering firm. His days at the office usually ended at five.

As I looked around my happiness for my mama's good fortune momentarily left me. Something was off. The lights were off, there was no sound. Nothing to indicate that he was home or even recently had been. I frowned. If he was asleep I was going to kill him. It was our anniversary. He'd even reminded me about it that morning via text as I was walking out the door to get to work.

I walked to his bedroom and gently pushed the door open. It was extremely dark, that's how he preferred to sleep, and I couldn't see a damn thing. I opened my cellphone and shined it at the bed. Empty. I flipped on the switch and frowned at the confirmation. Empty!

"Rio!?"

I glanced around the corner to the bathroom door. It was open and no one was inside. I felt panic start to seize my chest. What if something had happened to him? What if he had been in an accident? With hurried feet I searched the rest of the house. He was nowhere. I pulled out my phone and dialed Elly's number. As I pressed it to my face I noticed an envelope on the kitchen table. My name on the front.

Elly's phone went to voicemail. Shit, she was on her honeymoon. I set my phone down and picked up the envelope. Inside was an address and a key.

Quickly I Googled the address. A post office? I shook my head as I snatched up the key and headed out the door. It wasn't too far away but all the way there all I could do was wonder what this was about.

I stared at the inside of the post office, deserted at this time of night. I hopped out of my car and made my way inside. I glanced at the key. There was no distinguishing marks on it. Nothing to indicate the number of the box I was supposed to open. I pulled out the note again and turned it over. Nothing.

I sighed and looked up, studying each box. Something red caught my eye. I moved closer and saw that it was a piece of ribbon. I put my key in the box. If I was going to have to open every box I was going to start with this one. I slipped my key in and held my breath as I turned it. I smiled when the little door swung open and revealed a black wrapped box, a bright red ribbon tied around it.

I pulled it out and took a picture before I unwrapped it. He'd done such a bang up job. I smiled to myself, remembering the first gift he'd ever given me. It was the key to his house and he'd wrapped it in a wrinkled paper bag, complete with a staple on top to keep it shut.

Slowly I unwrapped the box, my heart was hammering so hard in my chest I was sure it was going to pop out. As I peeked inside the white tissue paper I saw another key. I frowned as I picked up the piece of paper, my hopes deflating. What had I expected it to be? A ring? More often this past year I'd regretted that I'd ever told Rio I hadn't wanted to get married. I'd tried dropping hints here and there about it but I wasn't sure if he was picking them up. I was going to have to be more direct. Maybe I'd have to propose to him.

I sighed as I noted another address. "How many more of these can there be?" I murmured to myself as I grabbed the old key and made my way back to my car. In the back of my mind I had a terrible thought that maybe this was a prank James was playing on us. I wouldn't put it past him to have me driving all over town just for the heck of it.

In the privacy of my car I Googled the new address. My heart was beating wildly in my chest. I knew that street. We'd driven down it last weekend when Elly and Kent had tied the knot. What could we possibly be going to do there? And what was with the key?

I let Google direct me to the house that I'd squealed with joy over only a week before. As I pulled into the driveway of the darling Cape Cod complete with a white picket fence I felt my heart rate quicken. The front porch lights were on, Rio's motorcycle was parked in front of the garage. My mouth went dry as I got out of my car and slowly made my way to the red front door.

My hand was shaking so badly it took me several attempts to get the key to fit into the hole. Slowly I turned it and stepped inside. I was accosted by the smell of garlic bread. The glow of candlelight led me to the back of the house and when I stepped past the foyer I saw him. Rio was standing by the candlelit table, he was dressed in a tux, red roses in his hands. His hair was slicked back, pulled into a tidy low ponytail. My mouth was watering at the very sight of him. I shook my head.

"Hi," I said as I stepped closer.

He met me halfway, a grin on his too handsome face. "Hi." He held the roses out to me. "For you, Princess."

"I should have changed before I came. I didn't know this was going to be a formal affair. Why are you all dressed up?" I asked as I took the roses in my free hand, briefly waving them underneath my nose. Our eyes met and I felt my knees go jellied. I loved that after all these years he could still do that to me. If someone had asked me ten years ago if we would make it, I would've told them no, absolutely not, but here we were and I couldn't be happier.

"You look beautiful just as you are." His eyes roamed my body, making it heat up. "Though you'd look better without all these clothes on, but we can fix that later. I got a call from your mom. She told me her good news." His eyes met mine once more before his head descended and he pressed his lips to mine. My disappointment at not getting to tell him the good news was forgotten the moment his lips met mine.

The kiss was gentle and yet so much more powerful than a forceful one. I groaned as I grabbed onto the front of his tux. His strong, steady arms held onto me, preventing me from sliding to the floor in a puddle of love-goo. He pulled back, still smiling and led me to the table.

I smiled as I saw the fresh pasta, the garlic bread, and the sparkling apple juice.

"You've outdone yourself," I said, my eyes drinking in the table. When I turned to look at him he was down on one knee beside me. I gripped the roses tightly, my breath leaving my body.

"Stacy, as the years have gone by we've been through a lot together. There were times I was sure you were done with me and you were going to kick me to the curb or find someone more deserving, but you haven't. I know that without you I am only half as good as I am when you are with me. I hope that I do the same for you. You light up my life, you make it worth living. And living is what I want to do, with you, forever. I love you." He paused long enough to draw out a box from his pocket and hold it up to me. He opened it and a diamond twinkled from the black enclosure. "Stacy Opal Hammond, will you marry me?"

Without a moment's hesitation I threw myself at him, wrapping my arms around his neck. We landed on the floor, his grunt rumbling my chest. "Yes!" I held onto his face as I kissed him. He kissed me back, the heat between us hot enough to melt iron. He rolled us over and pinned me to the floor.

"I cannot wait to make you mine forever."

"You don't have to wait," I said, "I'm already yours forever."